TEENAGE MUTANT
NINJA TURTLES
OUT OF THE SHADOWS

THE DELUXE
MOVIE NOVELIZATION

Published in the United States by Random House Children's Books, a division of Penguin Random House LLC, 1745 Broadway, New York, NY 10019, and in Canada by Penguin Random House Canada Limited, Toronto. Random House and the colophon are registered trademarks of Penguin Random House LLC.

randomhousekids.com

ISBN 978-1-101-93919-2

Printed in the United States of America
10 9 8 7 6 5 4 3 2 1

TEENAGE MUTANT NINJA TURTLES

OUT OF THE SHADOWS

THE DELUXE MOVIE NOVELIZATION

Based on the screenplay by
Josh Appelbaum and **André Nemec**

Adapted by **David Lewman**

RANDOM HOUSE 🏠 NEW YORK

CHAPTER 1

On Halloween night, the streets of New York City were even crazier than usual. Thousands of people dressed in costumes swarmed the sidewalks to watch the parade, laughing and cheering.

And Michelangelo, just this once, wanted to be a part of that craziness.

The giant teenaged turtle was tired of living in the sewers deep below the city with his brothers. He wanted to get a taste of what life was like for a normal person. And Halloween seemed to be the perfect night to get that taste. *Everyone* looked weird!

Mikey stepped out of the billowing steam rising from the sewer into the full light of the Halloween parade. Immediately, he slipped on a patch of black ice. Then he took a deep breath to calm down before plunging into the crowd. "Okay," he told himself. "You got this."

His three brothers did not think Mikey's parade visit was a good idea.

Leonardo called, "Mikey!" He tried to snag his brother with a lasso, but Michelangelo sidestepped the snare.

An oversized car circled Mikey. The car turned out to be a man in an amazing costume. Mikey stared at the costumed man, astonished.

"Nice costume, bro!" the man said to Mikey.

Mikey high-fived the man and marched on through the noisy crowd with more confidence. Near his right foot, a manhole cover rose slightly and Donatello peeked out.

Before Donnie could order his little brother to come back down into the sewer, Mikey stepped on the manhole cover, shutting it. *CLANK!* "What's the problem?" Mikey asked. "This is my city! These are my people!"

Giddy with the feeling of freedom, Mikey

leaned over and shouted into a nearby partier's bullhorn, "IS NEW YORK IN THE HOUSE?"

People shouted, "Yeeeaaah!"

A hand reached out from under the stoop of a brownstone apartment building, trying to grab Mikey's leg. "Get back here!" Raphael hissed.

But Mikey ignored Raph, easily jumping away from his hand. He yelled into the bullhorn again. "I CAN'T HEAR YOU, PEOPLE! I SAID, IS NEW YORK IN THE HOUSE?"

As everyone cheered, an eight-year-old boy dressed as an astronaut stared at Mikey and asked, "What are you supposed to be?"

Smiling, Mikey answered, "What do you think I am? A pirate!" He pointed to his eye patch.

A boy dressed as an alien said, "A pirate from the planet Freakazoid!" He grabbed Mikey's hand. When he felt its tough, leathery skin, his eyes widened. "That's . . . not a . . . costume!"

The kids backed away.

"No, no, no," Mikey said, holding up his hands. "It's all good!"

But the boys were terrified. As they ran off, the boy in the alien costume called, "Mom! Mom!" When he reached her, he pointed at Mikey.

The mother waved down a police officer.

Mikey quickly walked away, moving into the shadows. "I'm just trying to have fun," he said sadly. "Like everyone else."

WHONK! Mikey was yanked down into a sewer, and a manhole cover settled back into place.

Below street level, Mikey's brothers glared at him. "What part of 'ninjas move in the shadows' don't you understand?" Raphael snarled.

"What part of 'I'm sick of hiding in the sewers' don't *you* understand?" Mikey countered.

"That's not a saying," Raph said.

"I just said it," Mikey pointed out. "So it's a saying."

The four brothers continued their argument as they headed down the sewer tunnel. "The point is," Leo said sternly, "we can't be seen. It'd cause a riot. We don't exactly look like everyone else."

"Really?" Mikey said sarcastically. "Thanks. I

hadn't noticed."

"Guys," Donnie said. "We gotta scram. Tip-off is in five minutes!"

"Five minutes?" Raph exclaimed. "We gotta hustle!"

Inside Madison Square Garden, the New York Knicks were hosting the Los Angeles Clippers. The stadium was full of thousands of cheering fans, many of them dressed in costumes for Halloween.

"Let's go, Knicks!" Leonardo cheered. He and his brothers loved watching their hometown basketball team.

Donnie leaned over to Mikey. "You all right?"

"Yeah," Mikey said, nodding. "All good."

He reached into the thermal section of Donnie's backpack and pulled out a hot dog. Donnie hit a button on his forearm computer, and an automated nozzle emerged from his backpack. *SHPLORP!* It squirted mustard onto Mikey's hot dog.

Donnie smiled. "Does it get any better than this?"

"These seats leave a little something to be desired," Raph grumbled.

To make sure none of the fans at the game would see them, the four Turtles were sitting in the shadows high atop the Jumbotron scoreboard that hung over the center of the basketball court.

"Good seats are totally overrated!" Donnie asserted. He flipped down a set of high-powered binoculars, giving himself an amazing view of the game.

"Yeah," Leo agreed. "Who else gets to watch their beloved Knicks from this vantage point? Of course, I guess I wouldn't mind sitting courtside next to a supermodel. . . ."

Raph realized who *was* sitting next to the model. He pointed. "You see who that is?"

His brothers looked. It was Vern Fenwick.

Vern Fenwick was a cameraman for their TV reporter friend, April O'Neil. When the Turtles had captured Shredder, they'd let Vern take all the credit so they wouldn't be exposed to the public.

The beautiful model put her arm around him

and said, "You know, the other models are jealous you asked me out."

Grinning, Vern said, "Look, after the game, why don't we take Donald's chopper to the Hamptons for the night, grab a grilled cheese sandwich, and fly back by sunrise? I mean, YOLO, right?"

"YOLO!" the model squealed, delighted.

The Knicks took a timeout. Through the huge speakers came the booming voice of the Madison Square Garden announcer: "Knicks fans, please turn your attention courtside to meet New York's newest hero. He went from humble cameraman to being responsible for putting the city's most notorious criminal, Shredder, behind bars! Ladies and gentlemen, put your hands together for Vern 'The Falcon' Fenwick!"

The fans roared. The model gave Vern a peck on the cheek. "Go get 'em, Falcon."

Watching from their perch up on the scoreboard, the Turtles were shocked. "He gave himself a nickname?" Mikey asked. "How is he a falcon? Can he fly?"

"No, but he can swoop in and take credit for stuff he didn't do," Raph grumbled.

A sportscaster interviewed Vern. "So, Vern, tell the fans how a regular New Yorker like yourself was able to single-handedly do what no one else could—hunt Shredder down, fight him face to face, and deliver him to justice."

Vern knew perfectly well that he hadn't taken down Shredder alone, but he played along. "Well, I didn't do it single-handedly," he said. "I did it with a little help from a couple of friends."

The Turtles leaned in eagerly. Even though they'd made an arrangement with Vern to keep their participation secret, they were still hoping for a little credit.

Vern raised his arms. "Thunder," he said after kissing his right bicep, "and Lightning!" He kissed his left bicep. The crowd roared. Then Vern looked humble. "I believe there's a hero inside all of us."

Raphael scowled. "I got your thunder and lightning right here, pal!"

"I was just prepared to answer the call when my time came," Vern continued.

"So how did you prepare?" the sportscaster probed.

"Thanks for asking," Vern said. "Real unorthodox stuff. Carrying a railroad tie across my back and running through waist-deep snow. What any New Yorker would do."

"Not to mention all the dirty work done by the four of us," Raph growled.

"You know we can't take credit for bringing down Shredder," Leo pointed out. "Vern's just sticking to the arrangement we made with him."

"Yeah," Raph said, "and this arrangement has us spending the rest of our lives sitting in the nosebleed seats. Speaking of nosebleeds . . ."

Raph reached into Donnie's backpack and pulled out a high-tech pellet gun. He loaded it and aimed it at Vern, who was still blabbing about heroism. "So let me be an example that one man can made a diff—"

DINK! A pellet hit Vern's nose.

Vern looked around, trying to figure out what

had just happened. Trying to keep her interview on track, the sportscaster said, "We didn't quite get that, Vern. You were saying?"

Regaining his composure, Vern said, "I was saying that one man, and one man alone, can make a diff—"

DINK! Raph nailed Vern with another pellet, this time right in the ear.

"What the . . . ?" Vern asked, raising his hand to his ear and shaking his head. Imagining insects were stinging him, he wildly waved his hands around his head, trying to swat the bugs away.

The sportscaster decided her interview with this odd man was over. "Vern 'The Falcon' Fenwick, ladies and gentlemen!"

To a smattering of applause, Vern dropped back into his seat, humiliated. Raph laughed. "Maybe these seats ain't so bad after all!"

Donnie's phone rang. He answered it. "April!"

Mikey leaned in close to Donnie. "How does she sound? Is she asking about me?"

SHPLORP! Donnie hit a button on his forearm keypad, blasting Mikey in the face with mustard.

CHAPTER 2

April was in an elegant New York restaurant.

She was also in disguise: blond wig, business suit, and glasses. She spoke into her phone quietly. "Donnie, listen to me. I'm chasing a story for Channel Six, an undercover job. I was going through Shredder's police files, and I found a shell company he was laundering money through. A company run by Dr. Baxter Stockman."

Donnie nodded. "Lead scientist for the Techno Cosmic Research Institute—TCRI. I'm a big fan of his. The man's a genius."

"A genius who's about to find himself in a whole lot of trouble," April said.

"Do you need us there?" Donnie asked.

"Not just now. Stockman's a softie. But do me a quick favor." April opened a panel on her bracelet, revealing a tiny computer screen. "That birthday present you gave me? Can you run a remote download? I want to use the bracelet to access Baxter's email for the last few weeks."

"Sure!" Donnie said. "I'll do it right now." Donnie hit buttons on his forearm keypad.

"Thanks," she said. "I'll be in touch."

At that moment, Dr. Baxter Stockman's long black town car pulled up to Grand Central Terminal. Stockman's assistant, Trevor, parked the car, hopped out, and opened the back door for his boss. Dr. Stockman climbed out and entered the station, heading for the restaurant April was calling from.

April watched as Stockman approached.

"Good evening," the hostess said. "Do you have a reservation?"

"Jenny, it's me. Baxter. Baxter Stockman." She stared at him blankly. "I've eaten here every night for the past four months." The hostess still gave no flicker of recognition. "But that's neither fish nor fowl. . . ."

Having never heard this expression, the hostess said, confused, "The waiter will tell you the specials." She looked in her reservation book. "Baxter with a *B*?"

"Or maybe try *S* for Stockman," he said, "which is a surname, and traditionally reservations are listed under . . ." Noticing she wasn't listening to him, he gave up. "Or not!"

"Here you are," she said. "A table for one. Right this way, sir."

"Yup," he said a little gloomily. "Table for one."

As the hostess led Stockman to his table, April watched him check his tablet and set it down on the white tablecloth. She glanced at her bracelet. The screen read "WAITING FOR UPLOAD." Now all she needed to do was get close to Stockman's tablet. She took a deep breath and strode over to his table.

"Excuse me," she said. "Are you—"

Stockman was surprised to look up and see a beautiful woman speaking to him. "As much as I'd like to be someone in your life whom you would recognize, I assure you—"

"Baxter Stockman," April continued. "PhD. Graduated MIT at fifteen. One hundred thirty-three patented inventions by the time you were eighteen. Your innovations in mental robotics at TCRI have been a major inspiration." She cut herself off. "I'm sorry. I'm being a total nerd."

Charmed, Stockman held out his hand, inviting April to sit in the chair opposite him. "Please. Geek out."

"Big difference there," April said as she sat down. Once her arm was hidden by the table, she pressed a button on her bracelet. The screen read "UPLOADING STOCKMAN'S DATA."

"I'm a nerd," she clarified. "Not a geek. It's the difference between Lord of the Rings and Harry Potter. TED Talks and Comic Con."

"Sudoku and Lego," Stockman suggested.

April smiled. "You do know what I mean."

"I do," Stockman said, taking in her beauty. "I really do."

Trevor walked up to the table, glanced at April, and spoke to his boss. "We just got confirmation, sir. The package is shipping this evening."

"Make sure we're tracking it. Every step of the way," Stockman ordered. He gestured toward his tablet. "And, Trevor, I'm done working for the day." He smiled at April, wanting no more interruptions.

Trevor scooped up the tablet and headed out of the restaurant. April glanced down at her bracelet. The screen read "UPLOAD INCOMPLETE." Thinking fast, she pulled out her phone and pretended she was getting a call.

"Sorry, I gotta take this," she said, standing up. "It's my boyfriend."

"You have a boyfriend?" Stockman asked, disappointed. "Of course you do," he muttered to himself as April hurried away.

As she followed Trevor into Grand Central Terminal, April checked her bracelet: "CONNECTION ERROR—SIGNAL LOST." She had to get close to the tablet again. But how?

April looked down to Grand Central's main concourse. She spotted a group of girls dressed up for Halloween.

As she crossed the crowded floor, April took off her wig and pulled her hair into a ponytail. Passing a vendor, she tossed down a twenty and grabbed a plaid scarf. Tying the scarf around her waist like a skirt, April quickly fashioned a schoolgirl costume.

She plucked a cowboy hat off a passerby, put it on Trevor, and took Stockman's surprised assistant by the arm. She led him to the group of girls and announced, "Hey, girls. I found a cowboy!"

The girls laughed and surrounded Trevor. Still holding his arm, April said, "Look at those muscles!"

Confused, Trevor said, "It's nothing. I—"

"You know what time it is?" April interrupted. "It's selfie time!"

The girls instantly struck poses. April checked her bracelet: "CONNECTION REESTABLISHED."

"Wait a minute. Who are you?" one of the girls asked April.

"I'm . . . Jimmy's sister," April said, figuring

everyone knew someone named Jimmy.

Not this girl. "Who's Jimmy?"

"You know Jimmy," April said, stalling. "Karen's cousin." This girl had to know someone named Karen.

"Karen who?" the girl asked, looking suspicious.

April checked her bracelet: "DOWNLOAD COMPLETE." Success!

"Karen Fontolow . . . ski . . . berg," April said. "Everyone say cheese!"

"CHEESE!" all the girls said as the smartphone flashed.

And April slipped away.

In a hidden corner of Grand Central, April started reading through the files from Stockman's tablet. "All right, Baxter," she murmured to herself. "What are you and the Foot Clan working on?"

Then she found something that made her turn pale. "Oh my God . . ."

Back at Madison Square Garden, Donnie's phone rang. He answered it and heard April speaking urgently. "Donnie, I'm looking at the emails from Stockman's tablet."

"Just out of curiosity," Donnie asked, eager to learn more about his fellow computer whiz, "how does Baxter organize his apps? Is he a folder guy or—"

But on April's end of the call, the files started disappearing before her eyes! "Donnie, the files are disappearing! Some kind of self-destruct program!"

The screen on April's phone went blank.

"But I was able to read a few of his emails before they erased," she said. "And I was right. Baxter is working with the Foot Clan. And it's bad. Very bad . . ."

CHAPTER 3

"Shredder's being transported to a prison in upstate New York," April told Donnie over the phone. "Tonight. And the Foot Clan is planning on attacking the caravan to spring Shredder from custody! Unless—"

Mikey grabbed Donnie's phone and spoke into it, completing April's sentence. "—someone stomps down on the Foot Clan's plan!"

April winced at Mikey's goofy choice of words. When she didn't reply, Mikey sensed that she wasn't impressed. "Too much?" he asked.

"Just go!" April said, ending the call.

Shredder stood with shackles around his arms and legs. Armed guards marched him to a transport truck. Inside, there were already two other prisoners.

Guards shackled Shredder into his seat and climbed out of the truck, leaving the doors open. Standing outside the truck were the holding facility's deputy warden and a prison guard named Casey Jones.

"Jones," Deputy Warden Hamlett barked. "He's all yours."

Casey nodded and turned to Shredder. "What up, Big Daddy Lawbreaker? On behalf of the city of New York, welcome to the big goodbye!"

Shredder glared at him. Then Casey slammed the doors shut and smacked them with the flat of his hand. "We're rolling out!" he said.

Deep below the city, in the Turtles' lair, Master Splinter was meditating, balanced upside-down. His four sons barreled down the waterslide entrance to the lair, kicking up a big wave that splashed Splinter.

"Sorry, Master Splinter!" Mikey called.

"No running in the lair with wet feet!" he warned.

But the ninjas ignored him as they stormed past him and grabbed fighting gear. Raph dug through a cardboard box. "I can't find my throwing stars! Mikey, did you—"

"No, I didn't touch any of your sweaty stuff," Mikey said.

The Turtles raced across the lair, heading for their new customized garbage truck. But Splinter stepped in front of Leo, stopping him. "Explain," he ordered.

"Sensei, the Foot Clan is attempting to break Shredder out of custody," Leo said.

"If Shredder is free, his reign of terror over the city will begin again," Splinter remarked.

"Exactly," Leo replied.

"Then there is only one question: why are you wasting your time talking to a grumpy old rat?"

Leo smiled and ran off to catch up with his brothers.

"It's still a work in progress," Donnie warned from the driver's seat of their new Turtle Truck. "Lots of tweaking still to do, and then test-driving . . ."

"No time like the present," Leo said, reaching across from the passenger seat and turning the key in the ignition. *VROOOOM!*

The Turtle Truck powered down a tunnel straight toward a brick wall!

"Brace yourselves," Leo said.

"This is crazy!" Donnie cried.

Mikey sat in the backseat in a meditative pose, holding a throwing star in each hand. "Bracing, brother man. Remaining calm with the help of my lucky throwing stars."

"Those are mine!" Raph growled.

"Impossible," Mikey countered. "I found them in my room. And possession is nine-tenths of the law."

"Hand them over," Raph ordered. "Or my fist is going to be nine-tenths of your jaw."

The Turtle Truck slammed into the brick wall, which was actually a door—their secret exit from the lair. They burst through into an underpass below Grand Central.

"Shredder's convoy is seven-point-two miles east northeast," Leo said, consulting a handheld tracking device.

The Turtle Truck screamed around a corner into the night.

The prisoner transport truck headed down a highway. In the front seat, Casey was telling the bored driver all about a hockey game he'd played in. "The other team's on a breakaway, bringing the puck down the ice. I'm thinking, 'It's all you, Casey Jones!' They attack the goal. So I dig in my skates and—"

The driver reached over and turned up the volume on the radio.

Casey tried not to show his annoyance. "I get it. Hockey's not for everyone. It's an acquired taste."

In the back of the truck, behind the wire

mesh barrier separating the prisoners from the driver, one of the heavily muscled prisoners spoke to Shredder. "Mr. Shredder, I'm a big fan of your work. Especially the early stuff."

"I'm Bebop," the other prisoner told Shredder. "That's Rocksteady. I know the name's a little weird. His ancestors were from Finland."

"I'm Finnish!" Rocksteady said proudly. "As in, when I start a beat-down, I always finish it."

Bebop bumped his fist against Rocksteady's. "My man!"

"My man!" Rocksteady answered. They both laughed.

Bebop asked, "Where'd you get the nickname Shredder?"

"You snowboard?" Rocksteady guessed.

Shredder said nothing.

"No, you're right," Rocksteady said. "Better to not know. Don't wanna see how the sausage is made."

Casey turned and spoke to Bebop and Rocksteady through the wire mesh. "Tell me, how does it feel to have one brain cell between the two of you? Are there custody issues?"

"We gotta share a cell?" Bebop asked, confused.

"He said *brain* cell, moron," Rocksteady explained.

"Oh, so now you're a nuclear physicist?" Bebop asked sarcastically.

Casey looked at Shredder and grinned. "World works in mysterious ways, doesn't it, Shredder? You're gonna be spending the rest of your life behind bars with these two."

Under his breath, Shredder murmured confidently, "Or not."

At that moment, a dozen Foot Clan rode up on sleek motorcycles, surrounding the prisoner convoy. The Foot slapped magnetic explosives to the trucks' bumpers and . . . *BOOM!*

In the transport truck's cab, Casey grabbed the walkie-talkie. "We need immediate backup!"

Outside, Foot Soldiers leaped from their motorcycles onto the truck, clamping on with magnetic gear. As they began using lasers to cut through the truck's heavy armor, headlights suddenly flooded the scene. The Turtles had arrived!

"There they are!" Donnie cried. "And the Foot Clan's already trying to break Shredder out!"

"We'll see about that," Leo said calmly, hitting a switch on the center console of the Turtle Truck. Manhole covers fired from the truck's front grille. They slammed into the Foot Clan's motorcycles, sending them flying. One Foot Soldier dropped back near the truck to deploy a spiked chain.

"Incoming!" Raph called, spotting the chain.

"Reeling him in," Leo said, toggling a switch to magnetize a manhole cover and catch the chain. He hit another switch to pull the chain in, but nothing happened. "Donnie!"

"Sorry," Donnie said, reaching under the dash and pulling out a tangle of wires with unconnected ends. "I told you the truck's still a work in progress!"

Donnie manually sparked the wires together. A Foot Soldier on a three-wheeler drew closer, pulling out a buzz saw and aiming for the truck's tires! Donnie hit another switch. The walls of the truck dropped down, revealing a pair of large mechanical arms, one on each side. The mechanical arms opened up and spun a pair of oversized *nunchakus.*

"*Nunchakus giganticus!*" Mikey shouted. He used a pair of joysticks to control the arms. The *nunchakus* swept through the air, slamming into the Foot Soldier's three-wheeler and swatting it off the road like a bug! "Yeah! A direct hit!"

Mikey lifted the mechanical arms as if raising the roof in celebration. *WHAM!* The arms hit an overhead sign and broke off!

"Dude!" Donnie cried.

"Sorry," Mikey said.

A Foot Clan helicopter dropped down out of the night sky. On top of the transport truck, the Foot finished laser-cutting through the armor. The helicopter lowered an industrial magnet, which the Foot attached to the truck's roof. The helicopter flew forward, first lifting the truck's back wheels off the ground and then ripping the roof off!

On their turbo-powered motorcycles, the Foot turned and raced toward the Turtle Truck. They tossed hand grenades. *BOOM! BOOM!* The truck was rocked!

"Let's bring the ruckus!" Raph cried, backflipping out of the truck. As he twisted through the air, he clotheslined two Foot riders off their bikes. Raph landed, straddling a third, whom he then booted off the bike.

In the transport truck, Casey held on for dear life. Through the windshield he saw what looked like a souped-up garbage truck with TARTARUGA BROTHERS written on the side. *Who are* they? he wondered.

Above the roofless truck, the Foot lowered a rescue harness from the helicopter. The transport driver swerved hard, trying to keep the harness out of Shredder's hands. "Secure the prisoners!" he shouted to Casey.

Casey unholstered a Taser and slammed through the metal gate to the rear of the truck. Already free from his shackles, Shredder reached for the dangling harness. As Casey fired the Taser at Shredder, Rocksteady knocked the weapon away from him. The Taser's electrodes sailed wide.

"You owe us one," Rocksteady said to Shredder. "Don't forget our names—Bebop and Rocksteady."

Casey turned on Rocksteady and Bebop, drawing a pair of brass knuckle bowie knives from sheaths strapped to his thighs. "Bebop and Rocksteady," he said, "meet my closest friends, Biggie and Tupac!" He held up the knives for them to see as he moved in on them.

Bebop swung his powerful legs up and locked them around Casey. He pulled the guard toward him and slammed his face with a vicious headbutt. Casey was knocked out cold.

Bebop and Rocksteady grabbed Casey's keys and unlocked their shackles. Rocksteady headed forward into the truck's cab, and Bebop took

Casey's knives, appreciating their heft and gleam.

Rocksteady tossed the driver out of the moving truck and settled into the driver's seat, steadying the truck so the helicopter could hover above it and lower the rescue harness. Shredder climbed onto what remained of the truck's roof to grab the harness.

"I got him," Leo said, spotting Shredder. He keyed in the truck's targeting system. A pair of throwing stars shot out of the front fenders. They sliced through the harness's cable.

"It's all you now, Mikey," Donnie told his brother, pulling a lever.

Harnesses automatically strapped Mikey to his seat.

The roof opened. Mikey rose up in a gunner's chair, manning a twenty-inch cannon. But they were driving so fast, the wind blew Mikey's chair, bending and twisting it dangerously. "Donnie!" Mikey cried.

"Yeah, yeah, yeah," Donnie said, working frantically to bring the targeting system online. "Consider it logged in my engineering notes."

As his chair whipped around in the rushing

air, Mikey cried, "I don't wanna die! So much life left to live! Will never get to know how *The Simpsons* ends!"

Leo climbed into the back of the truck and used all his strength to hold Mikey's chair steady. Donnie nodded to him. "Targeting systems are online," Leo called up to Mikey.

As Mikey lined Shredder up in the crosshairs, a fly flew into his mouth. "YEEECH! GROSS!"

He chewed the fly and tasted it, and his expression changed to a smile. "Or . . . delicious!"

Shredder readied himself to jump up and catch the helicopter's landing skids. "One shot is all you've got!" Leo shouted to Mikey. "Take it!"

Shredder jumped. Mikey fired! The cannon's missile rocketed straight at Shredder. But then . . . Shredder disappeared!

"Where'd he go?" Leo asked.

Shredder gasped for air and looked around, trying to figure out where he was. Through a window he could see a strange, colorful landscape unlike any he'd ever seen on Earth. A mask appeared beside him, and a voice ordered, "Use it to breathe."

Shredder placed the mask over his nose and mouth. "Where am I?" he asked.

A large humanoid robot moved toward him. "You're inside a nightmare," the robot said. "But it's all very real. Not a dream."

"What is this place?" Shredder demanded.

"The last living planet of Dimension X." The robot spoke more forcefully. "Look at me when I speak to you." It grabbed Shredder by the neck and yanked his head down until he was staring at the robot's belly. From behind a panel, a pink, brainlike alien creature glared at Shredder.

"I know what you're thinking right now," the repulsive little blob sneered. "Of all the ways you'd like to kill me. But that would require you outthinking me. And no one—no *thing*— is smarter than Kraang. I have feasted on the blood of countless species. Rendered every planet in this dimension barren. But Kraang is thirsty for more. I need a new planet to consume."

Using its robotic tentacle, the alien known as Kraang activated a hologram of a spinning blue planet. "Earth," Kraang hissed.

"What does this have to do with me?" Shredder asked.

"Two decades ago, I launched an arc capacitor into Earth's dimension," Kraang explained, changing the hologram to show a large futuristic device being launched from a huge spaceship. "It would serve to open a portal big enough for me to bring my Technodrome—a war machine, if you will—through to your planet. But upon entering your atmosphere, the arc capacitor broke apart."

The hologram showed the arc capacitor breaking up.

"The largest piece landed in your Brazilian rain forest, where it still remains," Kraang continued. The hologram shifted to show a large chunk of the arc capacitor slamming through the rain forest canopy.

"A second piece plunged into your Atlantic Ocean, where the U.S. government recovered it."

The hologram displayed a U.S. Navy destroyer ship salvaging the second chunk. "It is on display in New York City's Hayden Planetarium, though they have no idea what it is.

"But one earthling has the technology to synthesize the pieces together—Dr. Baxter Stockman," Kraang said. The hologram showed Stockman working in his lab.

Shredder didn't hide his surprise at the mention of Stockman. Kraang grinned knowingly. "Heard of him?

"Your resources and your immorality make you the perfect agent for my plan of destruction. Retrieve the two pieces and deliver them to Stockman. He should be bright enough to assemble the arc capacitor and open the portal."

Kraang moved back a step and spoke with finality. "Failure is not an option. You will need a stronger army. This will make that possible." The alien handed Shredder a vial of purple ooze. "Build a better army. Open the portal. I'll see you on the other side."

CHAPTER 4

Back in their underground lair, the Turtles felt tense. With no idea where Shredder had gone, they needed to beef up their security. "North and east hatches secure," Leo barked.

"Infrared trip wires activated," Raph reported.

"Vent ducts locked down," Mikey announced.

Leo hurried over to Donnie's workstation, where April, Splinter, and Donnie were reviewing surveillance footage from street cameras. "Any hits on Shredder?" Leo asked.

"Nope," Donnie said as his eyes moved rapidly from one screen to another. "Nada. Bupkis. Negatory. Zilch. Zip. Zero." He stopped on an image and studied it more closely. "Diddly squat."

"So he just vanished?" April asked skeptically.

Donnie had an idea. "If I run the images from my shoulder cam through an electrostatic filter, we may be able to see . . ."

He manipulated the footage frame by frame. Just before Shredder disappeared, a halo of electricity appeared around him. "Look!" Donnie exclaimed. "Right there! It appears to be some kind of residue from a teleportation event!"

"*Star Trek*–style?" asked Mikey, who'd joined them.

"Beam yourself out of the way," Raph said, pulling Mikey back so he could see better. He asked Donnie, "Does that kind of technology really exist?"

April and Donnie exchanged a look. "Baxter Stockman's been working on that kind of technology for years," Donnie said.

"And his tablet was full of information about Shredder and the Foot," April added. "It was a virtual playbook."

"But the data you pulled off it self-erased," Donnie said.

April thought a moment. "Stockman must have a backup. I'm betting it's on the mainframe at TCRI. Donnie, can you hook me up with one of your toys?"

Donnie smiled. "I know exactly what you need." He pulled a small electronic device with a USB connector out of a drawer and handed it to her. "Totally plug-and-play."

"I can use my press credentials to get into the building," she said.

"Good idea," Donnie said, nodding. "We'll come with you. To offer support."

April shook her head. "You can't. The sun's coming up."

"Man," Mikey sighed. "It's like we're vampires or something. Without the cool ability to turn into bats and fly."

Moments later, as April emerged from the lair into the early-morning daylight, the Turtles watched her from the shadows. "Be careful," Raph warned. "Shredder's out there somewhere."

"I know," she said over her shoulder. "But where?"

April crossed the Channel 6 newsroom, heading straight for Vern Fenwick's office. She found him blowing into a plastic bag, sealing it, and placing it on a pile with several other bags, each marked BREATH OF THE FALCON.

"What are you doing?" April asked.

"This is a little side venture of mine—Falcon Breath," Vern explained. "People are paying up to two hundred bucks a piece for bags of my hot air."

"Seriously?"

"Supply and demand, April. Don't hate the player. Hate the game," Vern replied.

"Well, while you're playing games, I'm following a lead on Shredder," she said. "I need you to set up a meeting for me with the head of security at TCRI. Today."

"Shredder?" Vern asked nervously. "We're not going down that wormhole again, are we?"

"Just do it, Vern." April popped one of his Falcon Breath bags with a pen. She caught a whiff and immediately regretted it. "Ew. It's called mouthwash, Vern. Look into it."

"For real?" He huffed into his hand and smelled his breath as April headed out of his office.

CHAPTER 5

In the police department's motor pool, Deputy Warden Hamlett fired off orders for finding Shredder. "Widen the search radius to two hundred miles on all bridges and ports. And I want hourly updates from Homeland Security and Border Control."

"Make them on the half hour," ordered a voice.

All the police officers turned to see Chief Rebecca Vincent stride in with her second-in-command, Jade. "Excuse me?" Hamlett said.

"Bureau Chief Vincent. Organized Crime. This is my investigation now."

"I have jurisdictional authority," Hamlett protested.

"You forfeited jurisdiction when you lost three convicted criminals in one night," Vincent snapped. "Shredder is the most notorious criminal the city's ever seen. We had him. And now he's out there."

"Where did you recover the transport?" Jade asked.

"Under the George Washington Bridge," Hamlett answered reluctantly. He was used to asking the questions, not answering them. "It was abandoned and stripped."

"Any witnesses?" Vincent asked.

Casey Jones was still recovering from being knocked out by Bebop the night before. He stood next to his Dodge Challenger, answering Vincent's and Hamlett's questions. "Next thing I know, there are these ninjas on motorcycles coming at us from all sides."

Chief Vincent looked skeptical but said, "Go on."

"And then, in my side-view mirror, I spotted

a big garbage truck barreling toward us like it was on the warpath."

Vincent raised an eyebrow. "And what was the objective of this battle-hungry sanitation vehicle?"

"I was wondering the same thing!" Casey said. "When all of a sudden, these manhole covers started launching from the grille of the truck—"

"Manhole covers?" Vincent asked in disbelief.

"Yeah!" Casey said. "Like guided projectiles!"

Vincent and Hamlett exchanged a look. "You're taking some time off, Jones," Hamlett ordered. "I'm pulling you off the payroll." He walked away.

"What?" Casey called after him. "I'm not crazy! I saw what I saw!"

Vincent walked away, too, but Casey followed the two officers. "I can find these guys! I'm from New York. I know the streets better than anyone."

Vincent turned to face Casey. "First rule of tracking fugitives: don't take help from the person responsible for losing them in the first place."

"We were ambushed!" Casey protested.

"Thank you for your statement, Jones," Vincent said, clearly intending to end the conversation.

But Casey persisted. "Officer Jones. I'm gonna be a detective someday. Just waiting on the next enrollment cycle at the police academy."

"Good luck with that," Vincent said. "But for now, do yourself a favor—leave this manhunt to the professionals."

Her words hurt Casey. But he was determined to prove her wrong. He climbed into his Dodge Challenger and pulled a file folder on Bebop and Rocksteady out of his jacket pocket. He spotted something in a report. "So," he said to himself, smiling, "you two lug nuts have a few favorite watering holes, do you?"

Two motorcycles were parked in front of a downtown bar. Inside, Bebop polished one of Casey's knives as Rocksteady threw back a drink. "I really rattled that prison guard's noggin good!" Bebop said, laughing. "You see that headbutt connect?"

"See it?" Rocksteady laughed. "I heard it echo off the walls—*BOOOONG!*"

Bebop hit Rocksteady with a fist bump. "My man!"

"My man!" Rocksteady echoed. He saw the bartender approaching. "Hey, how's it coming with those sammies?"

The bartender set two pastrami sandwiches in front of them. "Here you go," he said. "Two specials." He slid two cell phones across the bar. "And your side of 'pickles.'"

Bebop and Rocksteady picked up the phones. "Untraceable?" Bebop asked.

"Those phones are harder to track down than Shredder himself," the bartender assured them. Bebop handed him a wad of cash, and the bartender walked away.

"How about the way Shredder just went *poof*?" Bebop said.

"You know, with him out of the picture, maybe we should set up our own operation," Rocksteady suggested. "Carve out our *own* piece of the underworld."

"Yeah," Bebop agreed. "And our own Foot Clan. How hard could it be?"

Still polishing Casey's knives, Bebop caught sight of something reflected in the bar's mirror. . . .

Shredder. And his disciple, Karai, holding a knife to the bartender's throat.

Bebop was worried that Shredder had overheard their conversation. "Shredder!" he called enthusiastically. "My man!"

"Remind me," Shredder said coldly. "Which one of you is which?"

"I'm Rocksteady. He's Bebop. I had the same problem remembering your name, so I came up with a rhyme—Shredder is better! You see?" Rocksteady said.

"Mr. Shredder, we were just talking about you," Bebop said. "Contemplating a consolidation of our criminal enterprises. We're thinking a fifty-one, forty-nine split. In your favor, of course."

"He isn't looking for partners," Karai said.

"Maybe fifty-two, forty-eight, then," Bebop

said quickly, still hopeful.

"I'm looking for errand boys," Shredder said.

Without missing a beat, Bebop said, "We can work with that."

"No shame starting in the mailroom," Rocksteady agreed.

In the Turtles' lair, Mikey and Donnie were playing a stacking game with a bunch of old refrigerators, TVs, bookcases, car parts, and other junk.

Raph paced back and forth impatiently. "We should be out there going after Shredder. Instead you're playing Junkyard Jenga!"

"As soon as the sun goes down, we'll be back in action," Donnie explained calmly.

Mikey freed the heavy piece of junk and started climbing the wobbly tower. "Do not belittle the greatness that is this glorious game."

In another corner of the lair, Leo confided in Splinter. "I failed, Sensei. You put me in charge.

And Shredder slipped through our fingers . . . again."

"I know it hurts," Splinter said consolingly. "But it's the price of being the leader, Leonardo. Sometimes you must carry an extra burden for the team. Remember: so long as you keep the team unified, you will always succeed."

Very gently, Mikey placed a rusty fender on top of the tower. "Who's the man? I'm the man!" In celebration, he started beatboxing . . . and the whole tower collapsed, burying him!

He popped his head out. "Best two out of three?"

In the downtown bar, Casey was watching TV. Chief Vincent was making a statement. "We're asking anyone with information on the fugitives' whereabouts to please pass it along to the proper authorities." Bebop's and Rocksteady's mug shots flashed onto the screen.

Casey glared at the bartender, knowing he was

being lied to. "I'll ask you one last time. You're sure they didn't come through here?"

"I don't know what you're talking about," the bartender said flatly.

"I love this song," Casey said, walking over to the jukebox. Casey slammed his fist through the glass and yanked out the CD that had been playing. "You don't mind if I borrow this, do you?"

"Hey!" the bartender said, crossing toward the jukebox.

"Never mind. There's a scratch on it." He whipped the CD into a neon sign, shattering it. "You really should go digital." He grabbed a mug off the bar and threw it at a cluster of bottles.

"You outta your mind?" the bartender yelled.

"Getting there," Casey said. He grabbed another mug and threw it at the bottles behind the bar. "Tell me where they are."

"I dunno," the bartender pleaded. "But I slipped them cell phones."

"And a businessman like yourself wouldn't sell hardware without a means by which you could track said hardware. Am I right?" Casey grabbed another mug and drew his arm back, aiming at the most expensive bottles behind the bar.

The bartender held up his hands. "You're right. You're right. Take it." He slid a handheld GPS tracker down the bar to Casey.

Smiling, Casey put down the mug.

CHAPTER 6

In his private lab at TCRI, Dr. Baxter Stockman kept checking the surveillance feeds from the rendezvous points he'd established with Shredder. "Where are you?" Stockman murmured.

The sound of metal on glass made Stockman wheel around to see Shredder scratching one of his metal blades across a glass tabletop. He was flanked by Bebop, Rocksteady, Karai, and several Foot.

"Sensei Shredder!" Stockman said, smiling. "The escape plan worked!"

"But not in the way you planned," Shredder said in his low voice. "I've traveled very far. There is work to do."

Stockman smiled as he listened to Shredder's tale of other dimensions and alien power. His research had already brought him into contact with Kraang. He knew its plans and hoped Shredder would be the one who could complete them.

April entered the lobby of the TCRI building and crossed to an elevator.

Outside, Casey pulled up in his Dodge Challenger, holding the GPS tracker in his hand. As long as they still had the phones sold to them by the bartender, his quarry had to be inside TCRI. "All right, Bebop and Rocksteady," Casey said to himself. "I know you're up there somewhere."

Baxter Stockman nodded, taking in what Shredder had just told him. "And Commander Kraang said this device will help open a portal to another dimension?" he asked excitedly.

Shredder nodded. "And when we do, we will

join him in dominating this planet. We'll have ultimate power."

"And indescribable glory," Stockman said, relishing the idea. "Think of it. To be responsible for opening up the fabric between two worlds!"

"I know what else is required to open the portal," Shredder said. "But those four brothers are still out there. We need to create soldiers that can defeat them with a single blow." He brought out the canister of purple ooze Kraang had given him. "This will help us do that. But first it needs to be synthesized. Which is where you come in."

Shredder handed the canister to Stockman. At the far end of the lab, through the blinds of a service door, April watched, shocked and concerned.

Stockman loaded a small sample of the purple ooze into a processing machine. The synthesized ooze came out the other end and was loaded into tranquilizer darts.

"Now all we need are test subjects," Stockman announced, handing a dart to Shredder.

Shredder loaded the darts into a pistol. "Candidates who will easily fall under my command. Large in size. Low in intellect."

Nearby, Bebop and Rocksteady were playing with a Bunsen burner. "Who do you think he's talking about?" Bebop asked.

Rocksteady said, "I don't—"

Two darts hit Bebop and Rocksteady. Racked with painful spasms, they fell to the floor and began to mutate.

Out by his car, Casey saw the weird purple light flashing in the upper-story windows of the TCRI building.

He popped his trunk. His hockey stick lay across his hockey bag.

CHAPTER 7

Excited by the transformations, Stockman rushed to his office, followed by the others. "Inside every human," he explained, "lies a dormant gene that ties us to our animal ancestors. It's as if that purple ooze is returning them to their rightful place in the animal kingdom."

Stockman and the others watched Bebop and Rocksteady. "This is gonna be good," he said.

"Rocksteady!" Bebop cried. "Ha! You look like a rhino!"

"And you're a . . . pig? With tusks?" Rocksteady said.

Bebop caught his reflection in a window and felt his tusks. "I'm a warthog, you idiot!"

In Stockman's office, Karai shrugged. "Makes sense to me."

Rocksteady thumped his chest and laughed. "Ha! I like it!"

"Yeah! Me too!" Bebop declared.

"It's time to get mean on the scene!" Rocksteady shouted.

In the office, Shredder turned to Stockman. "Prepare the entire container of ooze. We'll build an army."

April couldn't let that happen. She quickly scoped out the destroyed lab, noting the distance to the canister of ooze, the nearest exit, and a panic button for emergency shutdown. Then she sprinted across the room.

She punched the panic button, setting off alarms as the main doors began to automatically close and lock.

"Get that canister!" Shredder roared.

A Foot Soldier tried to grab April, but she slipped free. Two doors had slammed down, but a third was still dropping. April powerslid under it.

The heavy door nearly smashed down on her head, but April hopped to her feet. Looking back through the thick glass, she saw Karai, trapped on the other side and furious. April grinned and bolted.

Just as Casey grabbed his hockey stick and mask from the trunk of his car, he spotted April bursting out of the TCRI building and sprinting down the street. A moment later, the Foot raced out and chased after April. He recognized them as the same attackers who had run down the prisoner convoy on motorcycles.

Standing in front of the shattered glass doors of the main lab, Shredder addressed Bebop and Rocksteady, his new warthog and rhino soldiers. "Pack it up. We're heading out." He turned to Stockman. "Stay here. Cover our tracks."

He left, followed closely by Bebop and Rocksteady.

April pounded down a dark alley but stopped when she saw the Foot coming at her from the other end of the alley. She turned back, but the Foot surrounded her. She was trapped.

Karai stepped forward. "You shouldn't have run. I don't like having to run."

Hockey pucks flew in, knocking out Foot Soldiers! They all turned and saw Casey, wearing his old-school goalie's mask and wielding his hockey stick. He dove into the fight, taking on the remaining Foot.

Karai knocked the canister of purple ooze from April's hands. It rattled toward the end of the alley just as a police car screeched to a stop.

Two officers got out of their cruiser. One of the cops picked up the canister.

April took off. Karai shouted to the Foot, "She's seen too much! Don't let her get away!"

CHAPTER 8

April turned into another dark alley, but it quickly proved to be a dead end. She stopped and turned around. A Foot Soldier was at the open end of the alley. She was trapped again.

Then . . . *WHAM!* Casey blindsided the Foot Soldier, knocking him out.

Casey looked at April through his hockey mask. "I . . . ," she said, uncertain what to make of her masked ally. "Thank you."

Moving toward her, Casey shrugged as if it were no big deal to take down a bunch of ninjas with a hockey stick.

"What's your name?" April asked.

"Casey Jones," he answered. But his hockey

mask muffled his voice, so April couldn't understand him. He flipped off his mask. "Casey Jones," he stated clearly.

WHACK!

Casey was sucker punched by someone hiding in the shadows. "Get away from her!" a familiar voice shouted.

"No!" April yelled. "He was helping me, Raph."

"Who is this guy?" Raph asked.

"I'm . . . a vigilante," Casey said.

"*You're* a vigilante?" Raph asked.

"I'm a shadow of the night," Casey said.

"*I'm* a shadow of the night," Raph said with a hard edge to his voice.

"Technically, all of the night is a shadow," April pointed out.

A car's headlights lit up the alley, revealing Raph and his three brothers for a moment. Casey was shocked by the sight of the mutant turtles.

"You're coming with us," Leo said, reaching for April.

But Casey stepped between them. "Don't eat her!" he shouted. "We are not food. We are not your prey."

Mikey copied Casey's slow speech. "We know you are not a pizza. You are a slow-talking weirdo."

"It's okay," April told Casey. "They're my friends."

"Friends?" Casey asked, amazed. "No offense, but I hang out with some shady characters on Staten Island, and they're nothing compared to these guys."

Donnie tried to explain. "Our unique appearance is on account of having been raised in an experimental laboratory wherein . . ." Seeing Casey was utterly baffled, Donnie gave up. He turned to April. "You just walk him through it."

"First, walk me through what's going on here," Leo said to April.

"I went to see Stockman, but Shredder was there at his lab," she explained. "He was talking about opening a portal. And then he used this"—from her pocket, she pulled out a dart she'd managed to snag in the lab and handed it to

Donnie—"purple ooze to mutate these two big, ugly guys," she continued. "The prisoners that escaped with Shredder. You know, Warthog and Rhino."

As she spoke, Donnie extracted purple ooze from the tranquilizer dart and placed it in an analyzer on his forearm computer.

"You have eyes on Bebop and Rocksteady?" Casey asked.

"What do you care about those two?" Leo asked.

"I have a vested interest in bringing them to justice," Casey said. "Let's just say, in the last twenty-four hours, I've taken a crash course in taking down those two knuckleheads."

Donnie read the chemical report on the purple ooze. "I've never seen anything like this before. I need to run a more thorough analysis."

"All right," Leo said, taking charge. "Let's get back home. Donnie, take April through the alley. Mikey, give him backup. Raph, grab Friday the Thirteenth here and follow. If he can help us find

Bebop and Rocksteady, he's coming with us."

"Not a chance," Casey said firmly. "I'm staying right here."

"I'd agree with you, except you're wrong," Leo said, grabbing Casey's arm. "We share a vested interest."

Casey tried to pull away. "I don't share anything with you guys."

Mikey raised his hands, playing peacemaker. "Fellas, fellas! Clearly we are all simpatico when it comes to our desire to bring justice to the city. The people of New York need us to sort out our differences and work together as a single, cohesive unit. Which brings up only one question . . ."

He looked at April and nodded toward Casey. "Are you two guys, like, a thing?"

CHAPTER 9

Back in the Turtles' lair, Donnie studied the screen on his forearm computer. "If this purple ooze was injected into Bebop's and Rocksteady's bloodstreams, it's feasible that were I to pinpoint a microscopic signature, I might be able to use it to track their location."

"And if we find them, we find Shredder," Casey said. "Put them all in shackles."

"As long as we bring our hockey masks, what can go wrong?" Raph asked sarcastically.

Casey glared at Raph. "Seriously? Now I'm getting wardrobe advice from a bunch of swamp things living in a Chuck E. Cheese toilet bowl who call themselves by, forgive me, the most pretentious names ever? I mean—"

He paused, catching a glimpse of something emerging from the shadows. "Okay," he told the others in an urgent, hushed voice. "Nobody move. There's a HUGE rat behind you. . . ."

The brothers shared a quick, conspiratorial look. "Yeah, we've seen it around here before," Raph said. "There's only one way to get rid of him. Gotta stay low to the ground, and come at him fast and hard."

April said, "Casey—"

But Mikey interrupted, egging him on. "It's all you, Casey Jones! Go!" Then he stepped aside, opening a path for Casey, who charged forward.

Splinter whipped Casey's legs out from under him with his tail.

The Turtles laughed. "Good stuff, good stuff," Mikey said. "We really should have people over more often."

But Splinter was not amused. He confronted Leo. "You bring someone down here without asking me?"

"We're sorry, Dad," Leo apologized. "But—"

"Wait a minute," Casey said. "This is your *father*?" He shook his head, amazed by the sheer weirdness of it all. "Of course he is."

Donnie continued his analysis. "Dissolve the quadrant helix bonds. And reverse the cohesion. Wait. That would mean . . ." His eyes widened. "Is it really possible?"

At an abandoned pier on the West Side of the city, Bebop and Rocksteady were putting their newly mutated bodies to the test. Bebop punched a hole in the side of a shipping container. Then he turned to Rocksteady and bumped fists.

"My man!" Rocksteady said. "We're invincible!" To demonstrate, Rocksteady charged headfirst into a concrete wall.

Bebop snorted with delight. "My man!"

Rocksteady came away from the collision with a piece of concrete stuck on his horn. "Get it off! Get it off!" he yelled.

Bebop started to pull the concrete off

Rocksteady's horn, but then he felt the presence of Shredder nearby. Bebop and Rocksteady straightened up and faced their new boss.

"Master Shredder! Love the new digs!" Rocksteady said.

Shredder didn't answer. He turned to Karai and said, "I'm taking these two to go retrieve the first piece needed to open the portal. You recover the canister of purple ooze from police headquarters. At all costs."

Excited, Donnie approached Leo with an eyedropper filled with purple liquid. "Leo, you're not going to believe this. I made a solution from a sample of the purple ooze to expedite analysis of the isotope. But as I was waiting for it to catalyze, I started thinking. If the purple ooze can turn humans into mutant animals, perhaps, if properly reengineered"—Donnie dripped a small drop onto his forearm. Immediately the color and texture of his skin began to change—"it could turn us into humans."

Leo stared at Donnie's arm in awe. But after a few seconds, Donnie's skin reverted to turtle-green. "If we could get our hands on more of this stuff," Donnie continued, "it could be life-changing."

"We don't need that kind of change."

Donnie nodded slowly. "You're right. Being human could compromise our strategic advantage. We have a system that works. We shouldn't mess with the formula."

"Let's forget we ever had this conversation," Leo said firmly. "Most importantly, don't say a word of this to the others."

Donnie hesitated. He didn't like keeping information from his brothers.

"Copy?" Leo asked forcefully.

"Copy," Donnie replied.

But in the shadows, Mikey had overheard the whole thing. . . .

CHAPTER 10

In his office, Baxter Stockman played back the lab's surveillance footage of Bebop and Rocksteady mutating and April stealing the canister. Using video software, Stockman carefully began to erase portions of the footage. Just as he completed his task, two police officers entered.

"Thank you for coming," Stockman said, rising from his chair. "Forgive me, I'm still a little rattled. To think that on just a normal night, someone would be so bold as to break into my lab, my workspace."

He turned his computer monitor around so the police could see the edited surveillance footage, which now only showed April stealing the canister.

Stockman ejected a DVD from his computer

and handed it to the police. "It's a shock to say this, but I believe our intruder is that reporter from Channel Six, April O'Neil."

Casey headed across the lair, looking for a way out. April followed him. "You're not leaving."

"If I can just find my way out of here," Casey said, "yes, I am. I'm not gonna be an object of amusement to a bunch of overgrown pets."

"Casey . . . ," April said, trying to get him to stop and listen.

But he kept going, searching for an exit. "I was doing fine tracking Bebop and Rocksteady before you T-boned my investigation. I'm gonna find them or go down swinging."

Turning a corner, Casey spotted the Turtle Truck. He stopped and read the name on the side. "Tartaruga Brothers. This is the truck. It was . . . them? Fighting those ninjas?"

He turned and looked back at the lair, taking it in with a new appreciation.

"Those four have done more for the city than you'll ever know," April said. "And they'll never take credit for it. Wanna go down swinging? These guys hit harder than anyone."

Casey raised his eyebrows and then slowly smiled. . . .

That night, Shredder, Bebop, and Rocksteady quickly made their way through the Hayden Planetarium. They passed a display on the solar system.

"Hey, check out Uranus," Bebop joked.

"Check out *your* anus!" Rocksteady growled, offended.

"I happen to be wearing a very fine pair of undershorts," Bebop pointed out.

Shredder arrived at a massive piece of space debris. "This is the one."

His henchmen didn't respond. When he turned around to see why, Rocksteady was holding Bebop in a headlock. Shredder loudly cleared his throat. The two thugs snapped to attention and hustled over.

Shredder nodded toward the space debris. "Smash it."

Seeing a chance to get a little revenge, Bebop put Rocksteady in a headlock and tried to crack the space debris open with his fellow mutant's rhino horn.

But Rocksteady and Bebop just bounced off the hard object. Shredder examined it more closely, finding a swirl of symbols similar to ones he'd seen in the Technodrome and on the canister of purple ooze. He placed his fingers on the swirl of symbols, and the space debris swung open, revealing the large section of the arc capacitor.

"Now all we require is the other piece of the arc capacitor," Shredder said. He turned to Bebop and Rocksteady. "Ready to take a trip, boys?" He caught a whiff of their breath. "Pack a toothbrush."

Rocksteady frowned and held his massive hand to his mouth, checking his breath.

CHAPTER 11

In the lair, Raph bench-pressed heavy weights. Mikey was spotting for him. And reporting on what he'd just overheard . . .

"Then Donnie showed him it could really work," Mikey said, excited. "It was the coolest thing I've ever seen. It gave me . . . hope. We don't have to be trapped down here in the sewers forever!"

Raph racked the barbell. "But Leo told Donnie to keep it secret? From us? Who does he think he is?"

Raph jumped up and angrily headed toward the dojo to confront Leo. Mikey grabbed his hand, trying to stop him. But Raph was bigger and more powerful, and dragged Mikey across the lair.

"Wait, wait, wait!" Mikey cried. "If you tell

Leo that I told you that Donnie told him"—he slipped to the floor as Raph shook him off and continued toward Leo—"we'll never finish our hip-hop Christmas album!"

Leo was working out on the *muk yan jong,* a wooden dummy used for practicing martial arts. Raph grabbed the dummy, stopping its rotation. "Pop quiz," he snarled. "What are the three most important traits of the ninja?"

"Speed," Leo said. "Stealth. And—"

"Honor," Raph barked. "Where's the honor in keeping secrets from your brothers?" He hit the *muk yan jong,* sending it spinning back in Leo's direction. Leo blocked it.

"I don't know what you're talking about." Leo popped the wooden dummy back toward Raph, who caught it.

"Now you're adding lying to the list?" Raph demanded.

"If you're referring to what Donnie told me about the purple ooze, it's called compartmentalization of information."

"Suddenly you work for Her Majesty's Secret Service? If there's even a chance that the ooze could make us human—"

"We're Turtles. Whether you like it or not."

"It's not about what I like!" Raph insisted. "It's about what people out there are willing to accept!"

"Acceptance only comes from within," Leo countered.

Raph snorted. "You should consult for the fortune cookie industry."

"I consulted with Donnie. And we—"

"What about Mikey? Doesn't he get a vote? Think how much being human would mean to him! How happy he would be!"

"Only one vote counts," Leo said stubbornly. "Mine."

CRACK! Raph responded by hitting an arm of the *muk yan jong,* popping Leo in the chest hard enough to knock him to the floor. He looked up at Raph, incredulous.

Donnie and Mikey raced over. "Leo!" Donnie reported. "My listening algorithms picked up a distress call from the Hayden Planetarium. It may be Shredder. We need to get uptown."

Leo hopped to his feet. "You're up, Donnie." He turned to Raph and Mikey. "You two stay here."

"You're benching me?" Raph said angrily.

"Call it what you want," Leo said, starting off.

"What did I do?" Mikey asked.

Leo glared at Mikey and exited the lair with Donnie. Watching them go, Mikey turned to Raph. "So that went well," he said.

Raph paced back and forth, fuming. "The nerve Leo has. Big-timing us. Just 'cause he's fine with the status quo doesn't mean we can't make our own decisions."

Mikey looked confused. "What are you saying?"

"I'm saying there's more purple ooze where that came from," Raph explained. "And we'll get our hands on it." He stormed off in search of April and Casey.

As soon as he found them, he told them his plan.

"You want to break into police headquarters?" April asked doubtfully.

"Yeah." Raph nodded. "Donnie said he needs more of the purple ooze to track Bebop and Rocksteady. And you said the cops will have logged it into Evidence Control by now."

"Where is Donnie?" April asked.

"He and Leo are chasing down a lead," Raph said. "We're dividing and conquering."

"And Leo likes this plan?" she asked.

"I'm in charge now," Raph asserted. "Right, Mikey?"

Mikey hated lying to April, but he had to back his brother. "Right, boss."

Raph held up crude blueprints of police headquarters. "Mikey and I can go through the elevator shafts and air-conditioning ducts, but we're gonna need you two on the ground."

"Hold up," Casey protested. "I can't just walk into—"

"You wanna find Bebop and Rocksteady, don't you?" Raph interrupted.

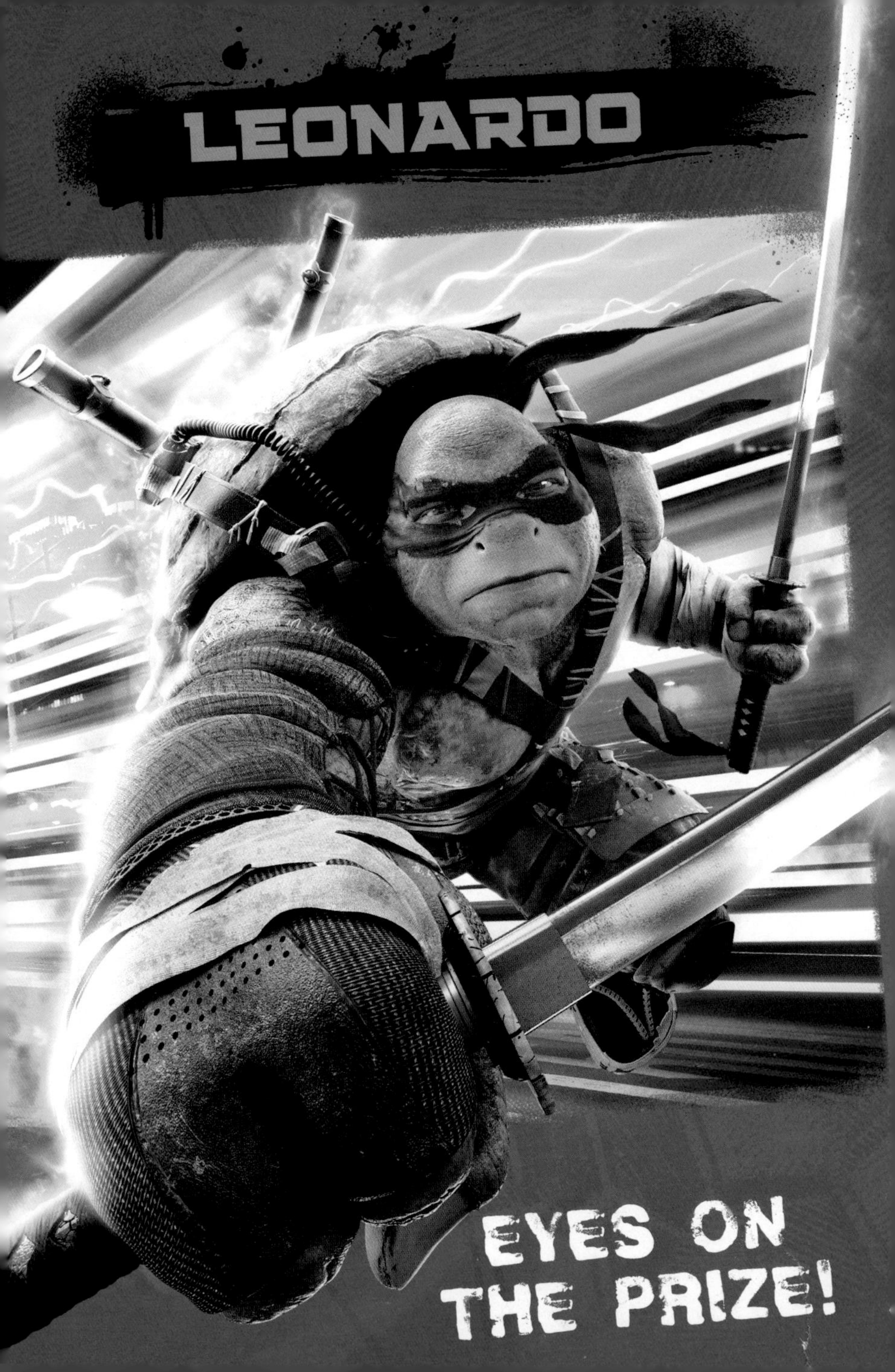
LEONARDO
EYES ON THE PRIZE!

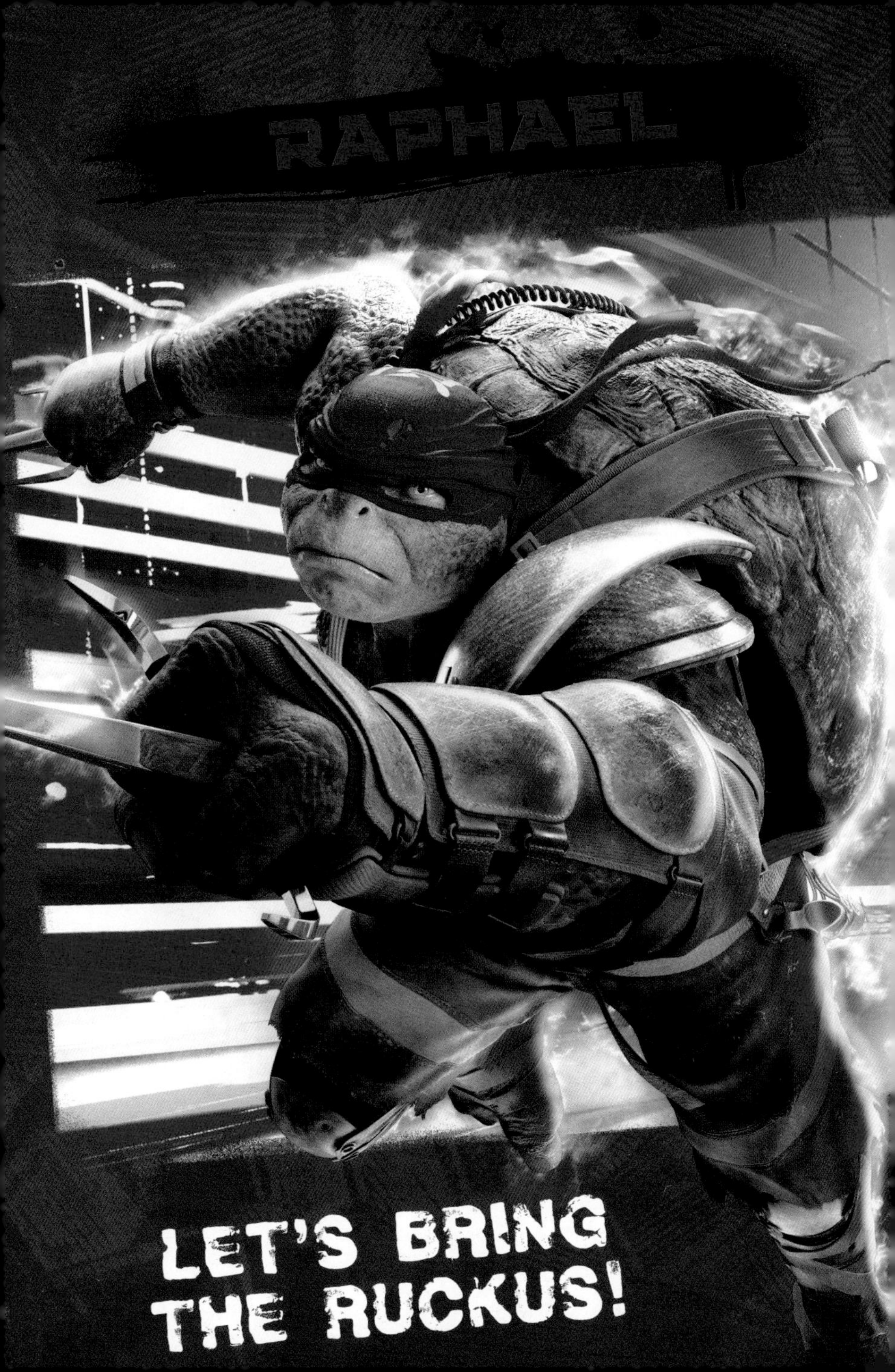
RAPHAEL
LET'S BRING
THE RUCKUS!

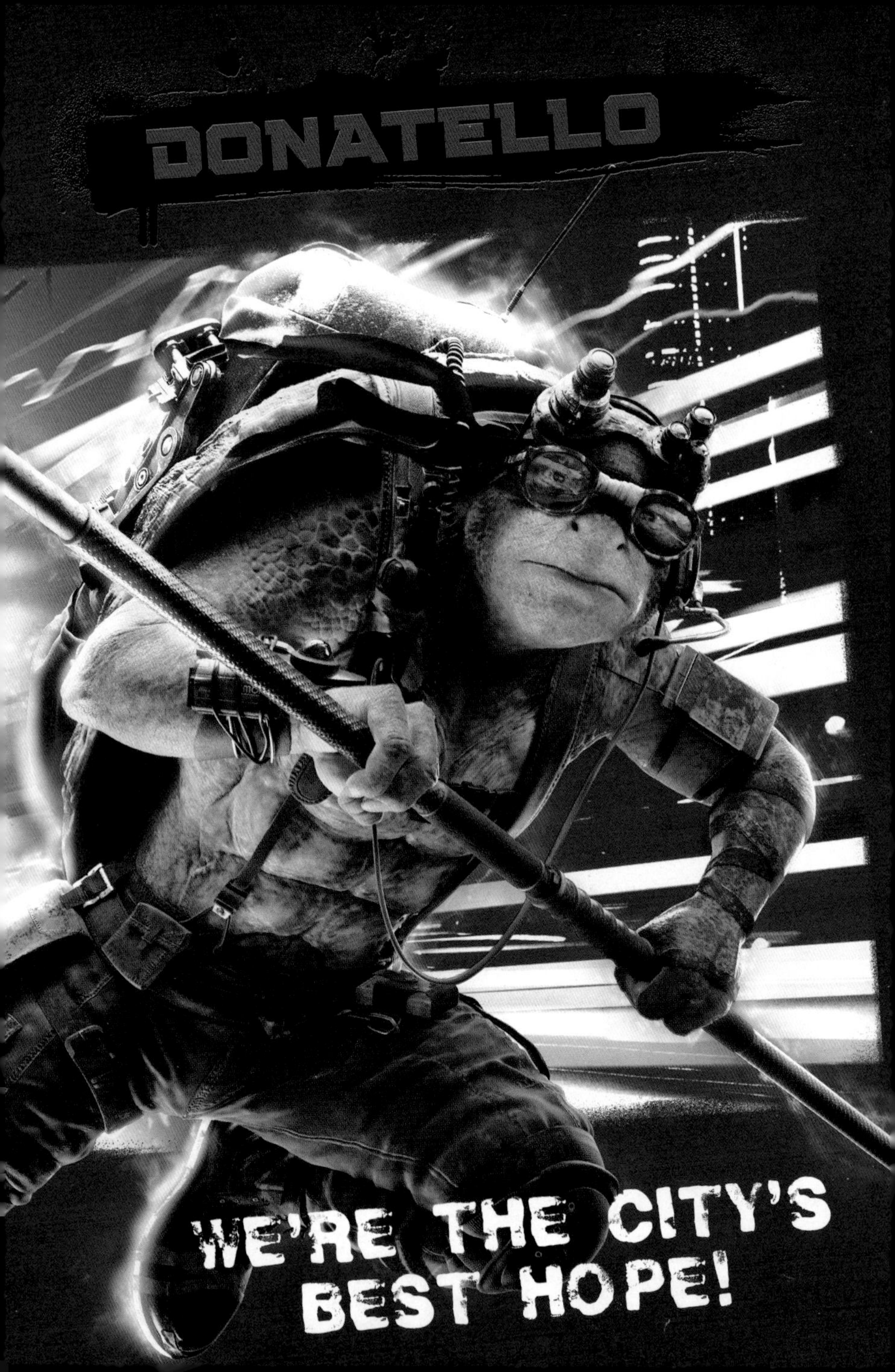
DONATELLO
WE'RE THE CITY'S
BEST HOPE!

MICHELANGELO

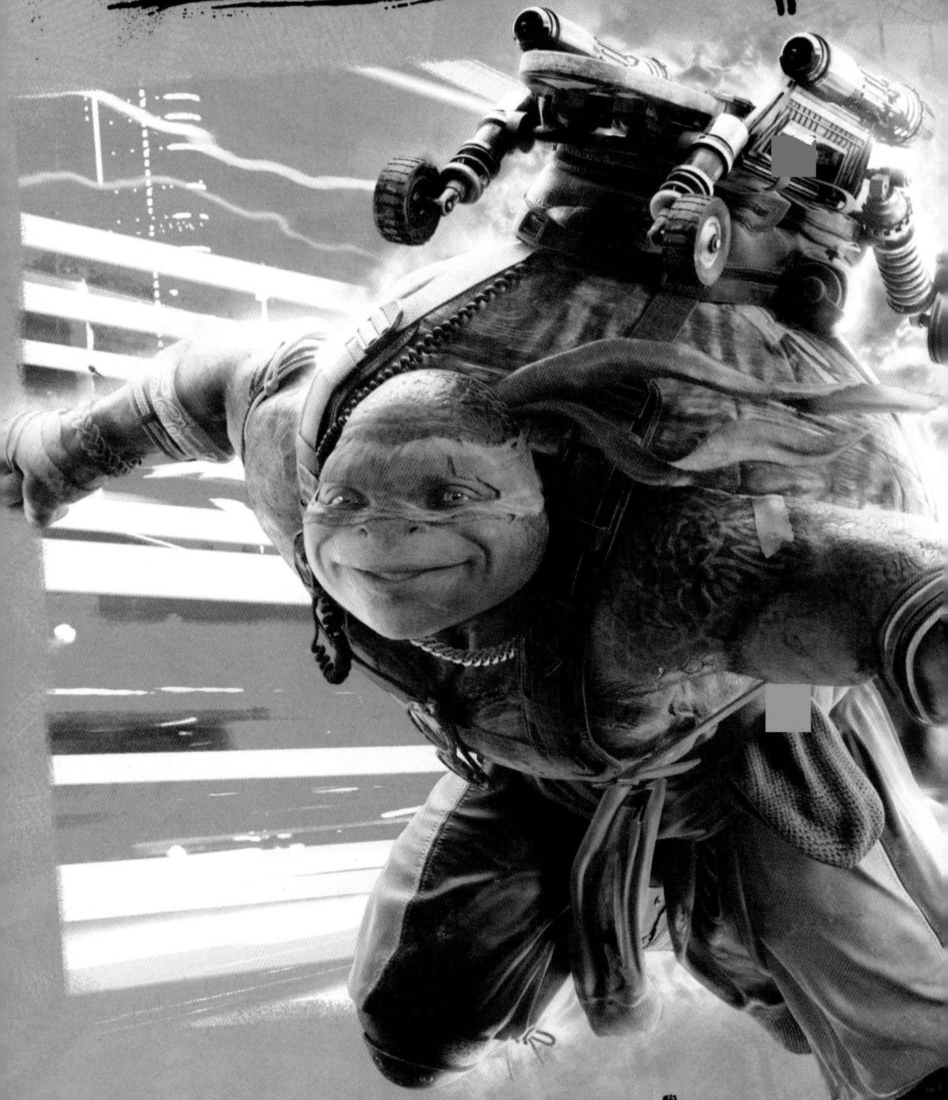

COMING AT YA!

SPLINTER

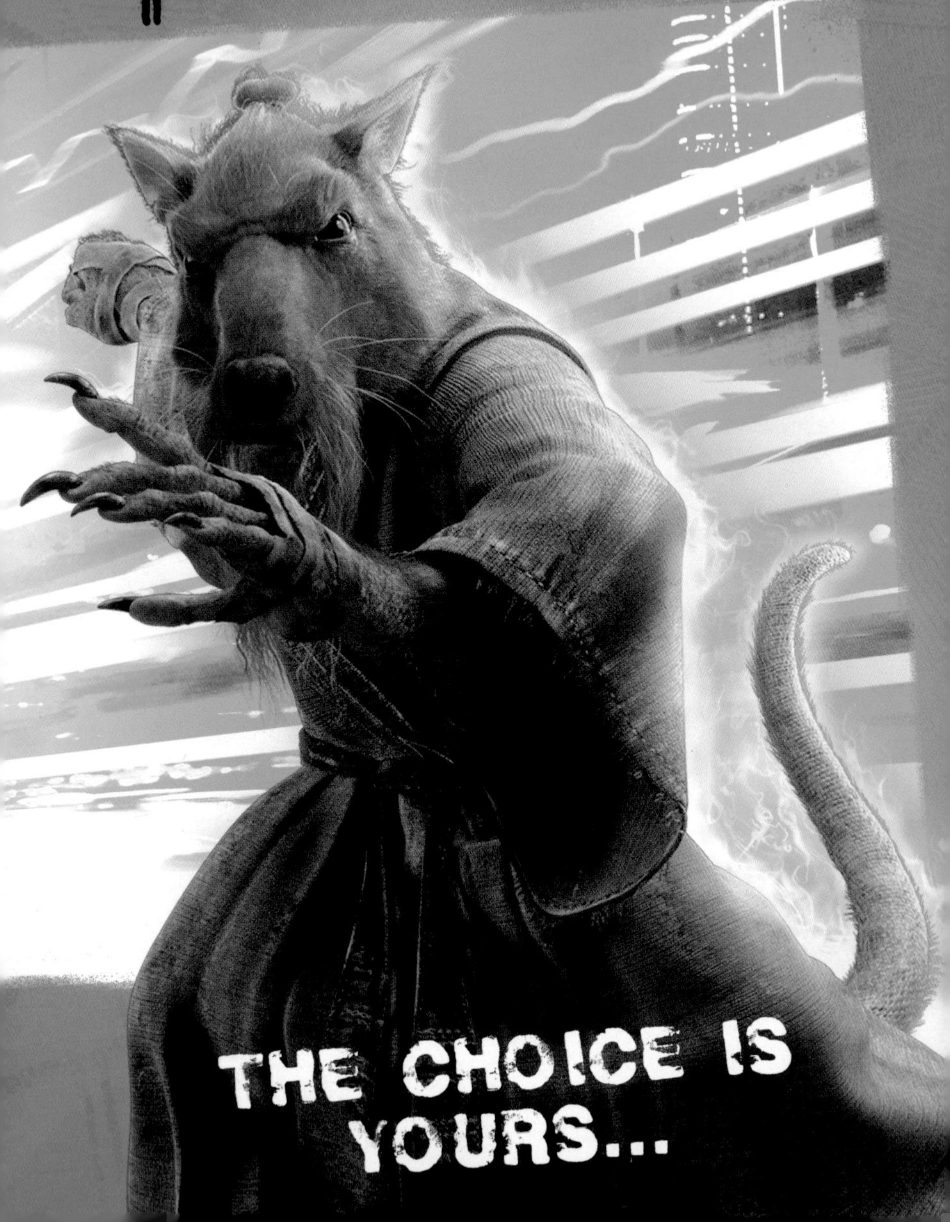

BEBOP & ROCKSTEADY

YOUR FACE

WE'RE INVINCIBLE!

"Sure, but—"

"But what? You chicken?"

"Who you calling chicken, Turtle?" Casey snatched the blueprints out of Raph's hand. "I'm in!"

Raph smiled, satisfied. "One more wrinkle: We'll need someone to get you guys past the first security checkpoint. The plan I've come up with may be a tad less than appetizing."

He nodded toward Mikey, who pulled out his tablet and played a video news clip. Over a photo of Vern, an announcer said, "Later this evening, Vern Fenwick will be honored by the police commissioner, who will be awarding him a key to the city for his heroics."

April winced. "Vern?"

Raph shrugged. "We work with what we got."

CHAPTER 12

At an elaborate party by the waterfront, Vern was thoroughly enjoying himself, circulating among the city's elite. Around his neck he wore his new key to the city.

"How does the Falcon keep in top physical shape?" he said to a beautiful woman. "Interesting question. It starts first thing in the morning, when I hop out of bed, hit the floor, and do a couple of hundred push-ups."

April swooped in, took Vern by the arm, and led him off to a quiet corner, away from the noisy party. "What gives?" he protested. "I'm the guest of honor here! I have a solemn duty to dazzle these guests with my charisma!"

"We need your help, Vern," April said.

"'We'? Who's 'we'?"

Raph dropped down behind them. "Having fun being prince of the city?"

"Go easy," Vern said to Raph. "First of all, *you're* the one who told me to take credit for capturing Shredder in the first place! Which, in light of him being who-knows-where, has me profoundly regretting our arrangement!"

Casey joined them. "Do we really need this blowhard? Can't we get in without him?"

"Who is this guy?" Vern asked, pointing a thumb at Casey.

Mikey appeared behind Raph. "Him? Total loser. Nice enough fella, if you like guys who can bench-press."

"Or fill out a T-shirt," Vern said.

"He's part of the plan," April explained.

"What plan?" Vern asked.

"To break into police headquarters."

Vern's mouth dropped open. Then he shook his head. "Look, this really isn't my thing. I'd love to help you guys, but I've got concert tickets. . . ."

"Look, Vern," Casey said. "As the resident new guy in this team of misfits, do us a favor. Just roll with it."

"Listen, new guy," Vern snapped. "I've *been* rolling with it. You have *no idea* how much I've been rolling with it!"

Raph had heard enough from Vern. "Police headquarters," he said firmly. "Thirty minutes." He strode out, followed by April, Casey, and Mikey.

As Mikey left, he called back to Vern, "It's a good plan! I'm proud to be part of it!"

In the Hayden Planetarium, Donnie stood on top of a huge model of Jupiter, looking around and admiring what he saw. "Wow, this place really is exquisite!"

"Hurry up!" Leo called to him. "The police will be here any second!"

Donnie somersaulted down from the big sphere, landing beside Leo as the wail of police sirens grew nearer. He adjusted his goggles and scanned the room.

"I'm detecting traces of Newtonium," Donnie said. "An ingredient critical for creating a controlled black hole. Which is the only thing capable of rupturing the space-time continuum. And you know what that means?"

He waited for Leo to answer. "Of course I don't, Donnie."

"From what I'm seeing, and the data I've collected, I think that whatever was inside this chunk of space debris may be the first piece Shredder needs to open a portal to another dimension."

Leo took this in. Then he said, "What I want to know is, if a portal opens up, what's coming through from the other side?"

CHAPTER 13

Raph and Mikey made their way across town, avoiding the crowds on the streets by traveling across the tops of buildings. As they landed on a billboard showing a happy couple skiing down a beautiful mountain, Mikey stopped Raph for a moment.

"Imagine it, Raph," he said. "If you really could blend in. Me, I'd rock the extreme game circuit! Travel the world, city to city. Maybe cross paths with April covering a story in some exotic locale . . ."

"Not enough action," Raph said, springing to another billboard. Mikey followed him. Raph noticed that the billboard held a recruitment ad for the U.S. Armed Forces. "I'd go Special Forces," he said. "Navy SEALs or Green Berets. Imagine what the military could do with my talents. Maybe I'd even form my own division—SEAL Team Turtle. Has a nice ring to it."

"Sure does, Raph," Mikey said dreamily. "Sure does."

Vern entered police headquarters and crossed the main lobby to the security desk. "Good evening, Officers! I think you know me, the Falcon. I just wanted to stop by and thank you, the men and women in blue working the night shift . . ."

As he talked, Vern secretly slipped a tiny transmitter into the back of the lead security officer's computer.

". . . for filling in the gaps, doing the work I'm not able to do. Hey, who wants to get a couple of snapshots with me? You know, to show the kids at home?"

Smiling, the police officers headed around the security checkpoint to pose with Vern. Across the lobby, April and Casey entered the building dressed as technicians.

"Ah, I see the perfect spot!" Vern said. "Right in front of that big NYPD seal on the wall over there!" He led the police officers away from the checkpoint, and April and Casey slipped past the group.

Inside one of the building's heating and cooling ducts, an icon flashed on the screen of a computer tablet. A homemade label on the tablet read "DONNIE'S COMPUTER—DO NOT TOUCH!"

"Donnie's gonna be so mad we're using his stuff," Mikey whispered. Squeezed tightly into the duct, he did his best to operate the tablet. The screen was loaded with automated prompts.

Raph looked over his shoulder. "Don't worry about Donnie. Just get it to work." He peered through a vent. April and Casey were stepping up to the officer at a security checkpoint.

"We're here to do a global systems interface update," she said, handing him fake IDs for herself and Casey.

"Hurry," Raph whispered to Mikey.

"It's not as easy as it looks," Mikey answered. "And it never looked that easy."

Touching the screen, Mikey worked his way through all the prompts and hit the Execute button.

The officer shook his head. "I don't seem to have you in here."

April's eyes darted to the vent high up on the wall. She gave her head a tiny shake. Raph saw her gesture and knew their attempt to hack the list of approved visitors wasn't working. "Mikey," he whispered. "Dude, think smart. Channel your inner Donnie."

Mikey desperately tried to follow the tablet's prompts. "I don't think I have an inner Donnie. I don't even think I have an inner Mikey. And I *am* Mikey!"

The screen prompted Mikey to hit the Execute command again. "Hold your breath," he said, "and hope for the best. . . ."

He clicked on Execute again.

At the desk, Casey tried to sound casual and bored, even though his heart was racing. "Well, dispatch just called our names in a few minutes ago. And the system's moving slow. Go figure, right?

Maybe try running our names through again."

The security officer looked at their IDs and retyped their names.

In the duct, the progress bar on Donnie's tablet reached one hundred percent.

The officer looked up, nodding. "Here you are. Seems we need updates everywhere." He handed April and Casey back their IDs.

"Seems so," Casey said briskly. "We'll be right on that."

"After we deal with this other thing," April added.

"Right," Casey said. "After."

The security officer opened the gate, and April pulled Casey through.

In the vent, Raph and Mikey high-fived and scrambled to the next spot indicated on their blueprints of police headquarters.

Vern crossed the lobby back to the security checkpoint, chatting with one of the officers. "Really? Nine years old with a sixty-eight-mile-per-hour fastball? That boy's on the path to Cooperstown! You must be one proud papa!"

As he chatted, and the police officers settled back in behind the desk, Vern smoothly reached over the counter, pulled the transmitter out of the computer, and palmed it. "Listen, gang," he said. "I gotta run. But know you are the inspiration that drives me to always put the city's needs before my own. Keep up the stellar work. The Falcon's out!"

Meanwhile Raph and Mikey were riding up an elevator shaft, standing on top of the elevator car. Mikey was humming the theme song from his favorite action movie, *Operation: No Way!* Raph glared at him.

"Tell me you're not loving this," Mikey said. "Our first heist!" He started to beatbox.

"Not now, Mikey," Raph said. "We gotta get an access card for April."

They jumped off the car. April and Casey were below them, inside the elevator. Casey gritted his teeth and blew out a series of short breaths. *SSS! SSS! SSS! SSS!*

"What is that?" April asked, grimacing.

"Getting my game face on," Casey explained.

"Okay, your game face is creeping me out."

"Sorry. Am I offending your delicate sensibilities?"

"'Delicate sensibilities'? I'm attempting a robbery in a government building!"

"Louder. I don't think they can hear you over in the mayor's office." Casey grinned. April tried to scowl at him but couldn't help smiling.

In the police officers' locker room, a young cop was changing into his uniform. He'd set his security access card on the top shelf of his open locker. He was unaware that two mutant turtles were above him. Raph was stretched between two ceiling beams. Mikey sat on Raph's shell, carefully aiming a modified blowgun. Raph's arms trembled with the effort of holding Mikey's full weight on his back. "Hurry up!" he hissed.

"You've got to hold still," Mikey whispered. "Why do I always have to do all the hard stuff?"

Raph growled. Mikey fired the blowgun at the security access card . . . and missed. He set up for a second shot. Raph's arms and legs trembled more violently.

At the same time, April and Casey rounded a corner into a long corridor. April indicated a door at the far end of the hall. "Evidence Control should be right through that door."

"Great," Casey said. "Directions to a locked door we don't have an access card to open."

"Yet," April said. "I'll get it."

"This isn't good for my heart—putting my life in the hands of four sword-wielding amphibians."

"They're reptiles."

"Oh, well, when you put it that way . . ."

Through a glass partition, Casey spotted Chief Vincent at the bottom of a staircase, talking to Jade. He stopped short and pulled April out of Vincent's view.

"Casey?" April asked, puzzled.

Back in the locker room, Mikey fired the blowgun again. This time the sticky projectile landed right on the access card! Mikey reeled it up, but as he pulled the card off the projectile, it fell from his fingers. He tried to catch it, but it kept slipping.

Just before the card fell on the young cop's head, Raph made a desperate lunge and managed to snatch it between his teeth!

Mikey silently celebrated, giving Raph a thumbs-up.

In the hallway, Casey kept his eye on Vincent and stayed back.

"What are you doing?" April hissed.

"Hiding."

"Why?"

"The woman on the stairs . . . I know her."

"But—"

"I can't let her see me!"

At that moment, Vincent finished her conversation with Jade and walked up the stairs toward April and Casey.

CHAPTER 14

As Chief Vincent approached, Casey whispered to April, "Quick—kiss me!"

"What?" April said.

"As a diversion," Casey explained.

"In a police station? That's your idea to draw attention away from ourselves?"

As they were talking, Vincent passed them. Casey slowly rotated, keeping his back to her. She never even noticed him.

Casey exhaled, relieved. April rolled her eyes.

Once Vincent was gone, April and Casey hurried down the hallway. Above them, in the ducts, Mikey and Raph squeezed their way toward a grate. Mikey made it to the end of the duct, but

Raph got stuck in the turn. So Raph flicked the access card down the length of the vent like a throwing star. Mikey caught it as April and Casey walked under the grate.

"Twelve o'clock," Mikey said through the grate, meaning he was right above them. He flicked the access card through the grate.

April caught it in her right hand and quietly said, "Cowabunga."

Now that they had the card, April and Casey just had to go through the locked door at the end of the hallway. But before they reached it, the Foot burst out of the evidence room with the canister of purple ooze!

As they made their way back to the lair, Donnie stopped Leo in the shadow of a billboard. "Leo, you should think about going easy on the guys. They were just dreaming. Don't you ever think about what it would be like if things were different?"

"Don't *you* start in on that now," Leo said.

"I mean," Donnie continued, "I would move out to California and get a job in the computer industry."

Leo smiled, softening. "Theoretically—we're just playing a game here—I always thought it would be nice to open a dojo. Teach the next generation the ways of the ninja." He looked away. "I guess I have been a little harsh on those guys."

Leo's phone beeped. He checked the caller and looked confused. "Hey, Mikey. We were just talking about you. You know, about before—"

"MAYDAY!" Mikey said frantically. "The Foot Clan has the purple ooze! We need backup at police headquarters!"

April and Casey chased the Foot into an empty office full of desks and filing cabinets. Foot Soldiers silently parkoured their way through the room, going over and around furniture without disturbing a thing. But Casey crashed his way through, shoulder-rolling over desks, knocking over lamps and computer monitors like a bull in a china shop.

April followed, making her way through Casey's path of destruction.

The Foot raced down a stairway, vaulting the railing at each turn. Casey tried to copy them but tumbled down the stairs. *"OOF!"*

Raph dropped down through a vertical duct. He saw the Foot toss smoke grenades ahead of them, disorienting the few police officers on overnight duty. The Foot had a clear path through the lobby and out the doors. Unless someone stopped them . . .

Raph turned to Mikey. "They're getting away. We got no choice, buddy."

Looking uncertain about the consequences of revealing themselves, Mikey nodded in agreement.

As Raph and Mikey ran after the escaping Foot, April and Casey fell in behind them.

Reaching the lobby, two Foot Soldiers threw

more smoke grenades and jumped the security turnstile. Suddenly, Leo and Donnie burst through a window!

Raph side-kicked the ninja carrying the canister of purple ooze and yanked it out of his hands.

Chief Vincent, Jade, and a handful of police officers ran into the lobby. At the sight of the Turtles, the officers reacted with horror. "Freeze! Don't move! Show me your hands!"

"No, no, no!" Raph shouted.

"What are those things?" the cops asked. "Monsters! Get on the ground!"

"We're the GOOD guys!" Mikey cried.

But Vincent wasn't convinced. "Take them down!" she ordered.

April shouted, "No! Don't shoot!" To the Turtles she yelled, "Go, go, go! Now!"

The Turtles burst through a window and disappeared into the night, taking the canister of purple ooze with them.

Vincent was surprised to see Casey. "Jones?

You gotta be kidding me!" Then she turned to the police officers and nodded toward Casey and April. "Book these two and hold them."

The police officers handcuffed April and Casey and led them away.

"What we just saw here stays within the department," Vincent told Jade. "The public doesn't need to know."

"I'm on it," Jade said.

As the Turtles entered the lair, Splinter barked, "It's all over the police scanners! You're being hunted! What happened out there?"

Leo snarled at Raph, "Tell him, Raph. You tell him how your break-in got us all exposed." He held up the canister of purple ooze. "And all for the most selfish—"

"The Foot were going to get their hands on that!" Raph countered.

"You didn't know that!"

Donnie fell in behind Leo, while Mikey

backed up Raph.

"Stealing from police headquarters," Donnie said, "has no scenario where you wouldn't get caught."

"Maybe if you hadn't lied to your own flesh and blood . . . ," Raph began.

"The way you lied to April?" Leo cut in. "And now she's taking the fall for your mess!"

The others were angry, but Mikey looked forlorn. "You should've seen the looks on their faces. It was awful. They weren't just scared. There was actual hate. They'll *never* stop looking for us."

Leo stormed off. Splinter followed him. He caught up with his son in a private alcove.

"I *told* him, Master Splinter! But Raph never—"

"You underestimated them. Undervalued their point of view. You drove them to this."

"But you always told me that a leader must have conviction in his own instincts. No exceptions."

Splinter smiled a small, rueful smile. "With all due respect, my dear son, those are just words from an old man, read in an old book. This is the real world. And in the real world, you screwed up."

Still not ready to accept his father's wise words, Leo looked away and shook his head.

Over in Donnie's workstation, a computer monitor lit up. "Got something!" Donnie called.

Leo and Splinter hurried to Donnie's side. "What is it?" Leo asked.

Rapidly working the keyboards, Donnie said, "The computer's pinpointed the isotopic signature of the purple ooze. I can find Bebop and Rocksteady's exact coordinates. I got 'em!" Then he frowned and cocked his head, confused. "Or maybe I didn't find 'em."

"You got 'em?" Leo asked, frustrated. "Or you don't got 'em?"

"I got 'em," Donnie confirmed. "It's just that they're at thirty-six thousand feet, traveling over five hundred miles per hour."

"Whoa!" Mikey exclaimed. "They've achieved the power of flight! Good for them!"

"They're on a plane, Mikey," Donnie explained. "And it looks like they're heading to Brazil."

CHAPTER 15

Donnie was right. A large military plane carrying Bebop, Rocksteady, and a heavy supply of weaponry was flying to Brazil to retrieve the final piece of the arc capacitor.

In Shredder's hideout, Dr. Baxter Stockman monitored the flight's progress on an array of computers. "They'll be on the ground in six hours." He turned to Shredder. "One step closer in our rise to glory."

Karai entered. "Master Shredder, we were blindsided by the Turtles. They have the canister of purple ooze. And they're working with an old friend of theirs—April O'Neil."

Stockman chuckled. "We won't have to worry

about *her* for much longer. I gave the police all the evidence they need to take her into custody."

At police headquarters, the mood was tense. "They're not monsters!" April insisted. "The real monster in this city is Shredder. And the two morons working for him."

"Bebop and Rocksteady," Casey clarified.

Chief Vincent shook her head. "If you think anything coming out of your mouth is going to add to her credibility, you are sorely mistaken."

"Shredder mutated those two goons with the help of Baxter Stockman," April said. "You need—"

"Funny you should mention Dr. Stockman," Vincent said, cutting her off. "We just finished analyzing security footage from TCRI. Guess who's on it?"

She picked up a remote control and pressed a button. On a monitor, Stockman's edited footage of April running through his lab played. April watched in disbelief.

"That's . . . that's not what happened," she stammered. "This footage has been altered. Edited."

Vincent shook her head. "We had experts check its authenticity. It's clean."

April felt trapped. Her eyes darted back and forth, as though she were looking for a means of escape. But in fact, the wheels in her brain were turning rapidly. "Stockman's a scientist. And scientists rely on redundancies. Especially in their labs. He has to have a secondary surveillance system recording of the event. Footage he wouldn't have altered. You need to find that."

"Don't tell me what I need!" Vincent barked. "You do your job, and I'll do mine! Of course, it's going to be difficult for you to file your little TV stories from prison."

"I want to make a phone call," April demanded.

Vincent smiled a wry smile. "I hate to break it to you, O'Neil, but the phone system's been shut down by monsters breaking into our headquarters. Tell me, where are they?"

"I don't know," April claimed. "And even if I did, I wouldn't tell you."

"They're not the ones you should be chasing," Casey blurted out.

A plane carrying freight flew through the clouds. In its cargo hold, Leo and Donnie sat together in a darkened corner, separated from Raph and Mikey by shipping boxes.

"So when does the pretty stewardess hand out warm towels?" Mikey asked.

"Not down here, Mikey," Raph said. "Not for us."

"Especially now that we've got targets on our backs," Leo said pointedly. "Life the way it was doesn't seem so bad right now, does it, Mikey? Before you started getting big ideas in your head."

"Don't put this on Mikey," Raph growled. "I dragged him into it."

That irked Donnie. He said to Leo, "How many more years does Mikey plan on hiding behind excuses like that? He's not a kid anymore. He doesn't get a pass just because he's the good-time Charlie around here."

That bugged Mikey, big-time. He said to Raph, "Dude, for real, Donnie thinks he knows everything. He's just good around textbooks—"

"Enough!" Leo barked, ending it.

The four brothers sat in silence.

Then Mikey said through a cough, "Know-it-all."

And Donnie said through a cough, "Good-time Charlie."

CHAPTER 16

The large military plane idled on a jungle runway as an assault tank rumbled down a ramp from its cargo hold. At the controls was Rocksteady, and Bebop manned the tank's automatic weapon. The tank turned off the runway and plunged into the jungle.

Before long, following Stockman's directions, they arrived at the ruins of a long-forgotten stone building deep in the jungle. At the center of the ruins lay a huge piece of space debris, identical in color and texture to the one in the Hayden Planetarium.

Bebop aimed the tank's gun at the debris and fired. The chunk of debris was blown to bits, revealing the indestructible device inside it—the other half of the arc capacitor.

Rocksteady grinned. "My man!"

He and Bebop bumped fists.

In the cargo hold of the plane, Donnie's forearm computer beeped. He checked it, and his face took on an expression of great urgency. "Oh boy. Bebop and Rocksteady are on their way back to New York. They must have already retrieved the last piece they need to open the portal!"

Leo studied the hologram projected from Donnie's forearm computer. "Our plane's about to cross over theirs."

"Yeah," Donnie said, "with a three-thousand-foot separation. I'll plot a course for interception!"

Donnie remotely opened the plane's cargo door. The Turtles looked into the vast sky.

"We're . . . jumping?" Raph said uncertainly.

Donnie nodded. "We have to go now. There's only a thirty-second window of opportunity to intercept their plane." He jumped.

Leo had glanced away from the open cargo door. "Okay, Donnie, walk us through this. Give me varying estimates on the trajectories depending on wind speed and—"

"Uh, guys?" Mikey interrupted. "He jumped."

"He jumped?" Raph asked.

Leo shook off his surprise. "Okay, let's go. Fall in."

But Raph hesitated. "Guys, you know what? I'm not so sure about this."

"What's wrong, SEAL Team Turtle?" Mikey asked. "I thought you were jonesing to jump out of a plane!"

"I was! I am! Sure I am! With you! Triangle formation!" Raph said. He turned to Leo. "On your go."

"Commence intercept," Leo said.

"In three, two, one . . . ," Raph counted down.

They jumped. That is, Leo and Mikey jumped. Raph faked them out, staying behind. As his brothers power-dove toward Bebop and

Rocksteady's plane, Raphael held on to the edge of the open cargo door, feeling a little guilty and a lot queasy.

Below him, Mikey was trying out his new rocket-propelled skateboard! He flipped, spun, carved, and soared high above the Brazilian jungle.

In the leader's spot, Donnie was hurtling toward Bebop and Rocksteady's plane, the distance between himself and the plane narrowing rapidly. At the last possible second, he fired a grappling line with a magnetic hook. *CLANK!* It stuck to the rear of the plane. But Donnie was coming in too fast!

Holding on to the cable, Donnie slingshotted around the plane, landing topside after one full revolution, ending up on the spot he'd originally aimed for. "Whew!" he gasped.

But above him, Leo was panicking as he tried to steady himself. Based on his current flight path, it was clear he was going to miss the plane completely!

"Aw, no! I'm off target!" Leo cried as the wind whipped around him.

Then a voice asked, "Need a lift?"

It was Mikey! He came zooming in on his skateboard and bear-hugged Leo!

"Slow down, Mikey! SLOW DOWN!"

"Where are the brakes on this thing?"

Leo and Mikey landed shells-first on top of the plane and skidded across its surface, heading past the tail. "OUCH! OUCH! OUCH!"

Inside the plane, half a dozen Foot Soldiers were enjoying a little downtime. When they heard Leo and Mikey slamming into the plane, they looked up and then at each other. What was going on?

Donnie grabbed Leo's arm as he slid past. Leo grabbed Mikey's arm. They banged into the plane's tail. *WHACK!*

"Hang on, Mikey!" Leo shouted over the roar of the plane's jet engines.

Just as Mikey was about to break free and fly off, Leo grabbed his wrist and yanked him to safety. The three Turtles secured themselves to the plane with Donnie's cable and took a moment to catch their breath.

"Where's Raph?" Donnie asked.

Back up in the cargo hold, Raph stared at the military plane passing underneath. His window of opportunity was rapidly closing.

"Oh man. Okay, okay. Yes. Okay. No! I can! I can! No! Yes!"

He threw himself out of the plane.

Below, his brothers saw Raph barreling toward them headfirst, like a three-hundred-pound bomb! "It's Raphael!" Leo shouted.

"He missed the time window!" Donnie yelled. "I don't think he can land!"

"Isn't he coming in too fast?" Mikey asked.

"Looks like he's off course!" Leo yelled.

With the military plane's cockpit in sight, Raph pulled the rip cord of his parachute. Inside the cockpit, the pilots were startled by a loud *THWACK* as Raph slammed into the windshield face-first! He slid off the glass, drooling. The pilots were astounded. Had they just hit a . . . giant turtle?

Outside, Raph's parachute was sucked into one of the plane's jet engines! With all his strength,

Raph braced his arms and legs against the outside of the engine to avoid being sucked in and diced to pieces. Finally, the tangled parachute killed the engine. With no suction, Raph flew back, flipping head over heels until Leo grabbed him.

Together they swung back on the cable, landing on the plane's roof. Raph punched his *sai* blades through the fuselage, giving the two Turtles a solid grip on the speeding plane.

Forcing an access door open, the Turtles burst into the plane's cargo hold and swiftly sent half a dozen Foot Soldiers flying out the door. They hurried toward a large wooden crate. Donnie punched a code on the crate's keypad and pulled off a panel of wood, revealing the arc capacitor piece inside. It was secured in a tough, clear plastic case.

"Okay," Leo said. "How do we turn this gizmo off?"

"I don't know yet," Donnie admitted. "I just got here."

"Hey, Donnie, aren't you supposed to know this stuff?" Mikey asked accusingly.

The four brothers heard snarling.

Bebop and Rocksteady!

"Wow," Raph said to Donnie and Leo. "They're actually uglier than you said."

The mutant rhino and warthog were offended. "Who's calling who ugly?" Bebop spat out, charging forward.

Donnie clutched the arc capacitor piece as his brothers fought against the two mutants.

Raph pushed Rocksteady. The mutant rhino landed on the parked tank. He lined up the tank's missile launcher and fired at Mikey. Mikey hit the deck. The rocket just missed him.

But it didn't miss the side of the plane. . . .

CHAPTER
17

WHOOSH! A huge gust of air sucked Mikey off his feet, whipping him toward the gaping hole in the cargo hold's wall. But just as it looked as though Mikey was going to be pulled out of the plane and flung into the sky . . . *FTHOOOOMP!* His shell plugged the hole! A perfect fit! Feet and hands dangling, Mikey celebrated his luck.

Rocksteady wasted no time aiming the tank's machine gun at Raph and unleashing a firestorm. Raph dove behind a stack of crates as bullets ripped holes in the wall of the aircraft until it looked like Swiss cheese.

A section of the cockpit door was torn away. The side windshields were shattered. The floor and walls gaped open, and the pilots were sucked out! They popped their parachutes and floated helplessly away, watching the plane streak off, losing altitude rapidly.

With no one at the controls, the plane went into a catastrophic dive, corkscrewing down toward the Brazilian rain forest!

In the cargo hold, the arc capacitor piece slid past Mikey. He snagged it. "I got it! I got it!"

But he lost his grip on the slippery plastic case. "I ain't got it."

The case skated right into Bebop's hands.

Donnie scrambled to what remained of the cockpit and grabbed the controls.

Running against the walls of the spinning plane like a hamster in a wheel, Mikey snatched the arc capacitor piece from Bebop and tossed it behind his back to Raph. "Catch it, Raph!"

In the front of the plane, Donnie pulled hard on the wheel, trying to bring the plane up out of its nosedive. But the force of the fall was too great. . . .

Bebop charged at Leo, but the Turtle flipped

himself up onto the tank, which was hanging upside down, chained to its moorings. Bebop's fist swung past Leo and socked Rocksteady right in the face! *BAM!*

Leo shinnied down the barrel of the tank, but the weight of the hanging tank was too much. It ripped from its moorings and crashed into the cargo hold, pushing Rocksteady's horn through the plane.

Leo rolled out of the way. Then he slid like a baseball player coming into home plate, scooping up the arc capacitor piece! He shouted, "How you doing up there, Donnie?"

"Everything's great!" Donnie answered, frantically trying to gain control of the plummeting plane. "Engine Two is blown, the hydraulics are shot— Yeah, I'm doing awesome!"

Donnie jammed his *bo* staff through the wheel and pulled with all his might. He managed to turn the nose of the plane up, but this sent all the cargo sliding and smashing into the tail of the plane. With the tail damaged, the plane started falling again.

Donnie desperately looked for a place to land the plane. All he saw was dense green rain forest. But then he spotted something—a narrow ribbon of river running through the jungle. It might offer a better chance of surviving the crash. Donnie steered the damaged plane as best he could, aiming for the river.

What remained of the plane's tail section broke up in midair. Raph was sucked toward the back opening! Leo tried to grab him, but Raph went hurtling out of the plane!

"No, no, no!" Leo shouted.

SPLASH! Raph hit the water hard, skipping across the surface on his shell at high speed.

Using his *bo* staff, Donnie pulled the wheel back as far as he could for landing. The wings sliced through the tops of the trees. Donnie prepared himself for the water landing.

And as Leo and Mikey flailed wildly in the back, trying to hold on to anything they could, the plane headed straight for the river. . . .

CHAPTER 18

SPLOOOOSH! Water sprayed everywhere as the massive broken military plane hit the river. The wings snapped off under the force of the landing.

Leo, Mikey, and Donnie found themselves underwater, quickly swimming away from the sinking plane. One by one, they popped to the surface, grabbing pieces of wreckage to hold on to. Desperately, they looked around for Raph but saw no sign of him.

Finally, he surfaced. Raph climbed aboard a piece of the plane's wreckage and kissed it. "Thank you, thank you, thank you!" he called, thrilled to have survived jumping out of one plane and falling out of another.

But there wasn't time to waste on celebration yet. The arc capacitor piece was floating down the swiftly flowing river.

Bebop, surfing on a piece of wreckage, dove into the water, getting a head start. Leo dove in after him, expertly swimming underwater and passing Bebop for the lead. But as they entered the river's white water, the two swimmers were tossed around like corks, scrambling madly after the arc capacitor piece.

Leo dove under the rapids and spotted the floating piece. He got one hand on it but slammed into a rock before he could grab it.

Carried by the waves, Bebop snagged the piece and climbed onto a chunk of plane wreckage. He rode it down the river, calling, "Later, suckers!"

But Leo was close behind. He hopped up onto the wreckage and knocked the arc capacitor piece out of Bebop's hands. "Give me that!" Leo demanded.

"Hey!" Bebop sputtered, trying to catch the piece. "Back off, freak!"

Leo executed a flying roundhouse kick, sending the plastic case back to Mikey and Donnie. "Got it!" Mikey cried, holding it over his head. The rapids grew even wilder, sweeping the Turtles downriver.

BOOM! Rocksteady had found the tank, and now he was riding it straight at the Turtles, firing missiles as he came. Donnie was in the path of a missile, but Raph yanked him out of the way. The missile flew over the river and slammed into a tree, which came crashing down, just missing Mikey. He lost the case, and Bebop grabbed it. Leo dove at him.

BOOM! Rocksteady fired again. As Leo and Bebop struggled over the case, the missile cut a tree in half above them. Bebop managed to knock Leo away, but the tree slammed down onto the wreckage Bebop was standing on, catapulting him through the air. *"WHOOAA!"*

He landed near the tank with the arc capacitor piece still in his hand. Rocksteady leaped out of the tank and they pounded fists. "My man!"

A helicopter swooped into view and lowered a cable. The two thugs grabbed hold and were lifted up into the chopper, carrying the arc capacitor piece away with them.

Still in the rapids, the Turtles looked up to see Bebop and Rocksteady escaping with the piece. "We've failed!" Leo sputtered.

They noticed Bebop and Rocksteady laughing and pointing downriver. The Turtles were being pulled toward a massive waterfall!

Within seconds they were swept over the edge of the falls. They fell, inches from the wall of rushing water. Raph, Donnie, and Mikey quickly joined arms. But Leo was too far in front of them. They couldn't reach him!

Mikey whipped out his *nunchakus* and extended one end to Leo as they continued to freefall. Stretching out his arm as far as possible, Leo managed to grab the weapon. Mikey pulled him in, shouting, "Hold on! Hold on!"

Once all four Turtles were holding on to each other, Donnie pulled the ripcord of his parachute, slowing their fall. They breathed a little easier. But they forgot one thing. . . .

The tank!

It barreled over the top of the waterfall, heading straight for them. "YAAAAAHHH!" they screamed, certain they were doomed.

The tank twisted and tumbled past them, just missing them.

"Thanks, guys," Leo said, relieved.

BOOM! When the tank hit bottom, it fired up one final blast. The missile rocketed straight up, tearing through the Turtles' parachute, sending them plummeting into the water below! *SPLOOSH!*

CHAPTER 19

At police headquarters, every officer was intent on finding the monsters hiding somewhere in the city. And in the interrogation room, Chief Vincent was questioning April and Casey again. She sat across the table from them.

"It's been almost twenty-four hours," April said. "If you're going to press charges, press charges."

"And you owe her a phone call," Casey added.

"I don't owe anyone anything until you tell me where those things came from," Vincent answered in a steely voice. She got up to leave, but Casey stood and blocked her exit.

"New Hampshire," he said. "You happy?"

She gave him a long, hard look. "Wow, I'm impressed. You're actually an even bigger loser than I thought."

There was a knock at the door. Jade entered. "Chief, we need you for a briefing."

Vincent pushed past Casey and left with Jade. April realized Casey had been stung by Vincent's words. "Don't listen to her," she told him. "She's just trying to get under your skin."

"No," he sighed. "She's right. I've been hearing that all my life. I've had only one dream: to make detective in the New York City police department. I wanted to put criminals away, instead of watching them in their cages. But working in corrections, I learned two good things from being around criminals. One, that justice comes in all shapes and sizes. You just have to fight for it. And two, picking a cop's pocket is easier than you think."

He held up Vincent's cell phone and grinned. "Make your call."

April smiled and took the phone. She knew just who she was going to call.

In his apartment, Vern was taping a clipping into a scrapbook. The headline was WHEN WILL THE FALCON SOAR AGAIN? Humming to himself happily, he flipped through the scrapbook's pages, rereading all the articles. His phone rang.

"Vern," April said. "I need you to do something for me. Are you busy? What are you doing?"

"Um, push-ups," Vern lied. "Six hundred and eight, six hundred and nine—"

"Listen," April interrupted. "This is important and there isn't much time."

"Okay," Vern said. "Go ahead."

She told Vern how the police thought she'd wrecked Baxter Stockman's lab. "Stockman doctored the surveillance footage to make me look like the bad guy. But I'm betting there's a secondary feed that will prove Shredder's working with Stockman, and that the two of them created Bebop and Rocksteady. I need you to get that backup footage."

Vern frowned. "You mean break into

Stockman's lab and steal it? Sounds dangerous. Why would I do that?"

"Well," April said, "I just thought you might like a chance to actually be the hero everyone believes you are."

Stowed away in the cargo hold of another plane, the Turtles flew back from Brazil. Surrounded by live animals in travel crates, the brothers argued about their failure to capture the final piece of the arc capacitor. There were no sides this time. It was every Turtle for himself.

"You can't just push right past me," Mikey said accusingly.

"I can if you're being a nitwit," Raph said. "You were gonna lose the—"

"I had it in my hand!" Donnie barked at Leo. "You acted like I wasn't even there!"

"It's not my job to make your presence known," Leo argued. "Get out of your own head and communicate!"

"What'd you expect?" Raph asked Leo. "Donnie's all logic and no social skills."

"Coming from a guy who's all instinct, no restraint," Mikey said, pointing a thumb at Raph.

"What do you know about anything?" Leo snapped at Mikey. "You're all heart and no brains!"

"How could you!" Donnie said to Leo. "You may know a lot about strategy, but you know nothing about feelings."

The four sat there, stunned by each other's harsh words.

"Fair enough," Leo finally stated. "You know the one thing I am feeling? This isn't working. We're too different. We keep failing. The city deserves better. We may be brothers, but we're not a team. We should stop pretending we're something we're not."

Leo's words sank in. And they all thought the same thing: *Should we call it quits?*

CHAPTER
20

At the TCRI building, Vern walked confidently up to the young security guard. "Coming through," he stated with fake authority.

The security guard was thrown. No one had ever just walked up to Dr. Baxter Stockman's private laboratory and said "Coming through" before.

"It's . . . it's a restricted area," he stammered.

Vern made a face. "Restricted? I know one thing that will open every door in town." He pulled out a key hanging on a chain around his neck. "The key to the city!"

The young guard was definitely impressed. Then he realized who he was talking to. "You're the Falc—"

Vern held his finger up, silencing the guard. "You haven't earned the respect yet to say that name. You wanna put yourself on the road to respect?"

His eyes wide, the guard nodded seriously.

"Then run downstairs and fetch me a mochaccino," Vern said. Then he repeated, "Coming through."

He slid past the security guard, who hurried over to the elevator to go fetch Vern's mochaccino. Vern headed into the lab, looking around for the device storing the footage April needed. "Secondary surveillance . . . secondary surveillance," he muttered to himself. "Come on, Vern, you were a cameraman in a former life. Before you got fancy. Where would you—"

Vern zeroed in on a modern light fixture hanging on the wall. It seemed oddly placed, and it was the only one like it in the room. When he looked closer, he found a microcamera wired into the wall. He yanked on the wire, following it all around the room, making a mess as the wire ripped through the plaster.

He ended up right back where he'd started. He found a metal panel, pried it open, and saw a small hard drive. "Yes! Come to Falcon, baby!"

He grabbed it. Victory!

Hurrying to leave the building, Vern headed to the elevator doors. They slid open, and the security guard stepped out, carrying Vern's mochaccino. Vern took the hot drink and got in the elevator. "Keep up the good work. One day I may be looking for a sidekick. But for now, the Falcon soars alone."

He sipped the drink. "Ow! Too hot!"

The Turtles were back in their lair with Splinter, but no one was talking. It was unusually quiet in their home beneath the streets of the city. Each Turtle sat alone, thinking about their fractured state and what they should do about it.

From a higher spot in the lair, Splinter looked down, watching his silent sons, very concerned.

Inside Shredder's hideout, Dr. Baxter Stockman was concentrating on the important task before him.

An array of panels surrounded the pieces of the arc capacitor. All Stockman had to do was put them together and turn them on. With Shredder, Bebop, and Rocksteady watching his every move, he simply had to master a mysterious alien technology.

Easy, right?

He pulled on protective arm wraps and went to work, cautiously fitting the pieces together.

As the pieces clicked into place, the arc capacitor started to glow, dully at first, then more intensely, with brighter colors shifting across the surface. An odd humming sound grew louder and louder.

"It's working," Shredder said. His voice rarely betrayed any sign of joy, but he sounded deeply satisfied.

Stockman smiled. "We did it. Once it's powered up, the portal will open within minutes."

He pressed a cluster of alien symbols on the side of the arc capacitor. "I am ready for my close-up," he said quietly to himself.

As a ball of light began to form at the center of the device, Bebop and Rocksteady stared, completely in awe of what they were seeing. "We only need one more thing to make this the perfect victory—hot wings!"

"My man!" Rocksteady said, fist-bumping Bebop.

At police headquarters, Vern hurried up to Chief Vincent and handed her the hard drive he'd taken from TCRI. "Chief Vincent," he said, "you need to see this."

When Vincent saw Shredder and Stockman together, and the amazing transformation of Bebop and Rocksteady, she sent Jade to get April and Casey.

Moments later, Jade walked up with the two suspects. Vincent was still watching the surveillance footage on a large monitor. "Here they are, Chief," Jade said.

Without taking her eyes off the monitor, Vincent said, "Cut 'em loose."

She started to walk away, but Casey said, "Chief, you might need this." When she turned around, she saw Casey holding her phone, grinning. Scowling, she snatched the phone and stormed off.

Jade handed April and Casey their belongings, including April's phone. April caught Vern's eye. "Nice work," she said. He grinned.

Jade hurried after her boss, with April, Casey, and Vern a few steps behind. "Chief, should I contact Animal Control?" she asked. "For the rhino and the warthog, I mean?"

"I knew what you meant," Vincent said, still walking. "Don't bother. I think the capture of Bebop and Rocksteady is above your pay grade." Then she barked to other police officers, "I want an all-points bulletin out on Dr. Baxter Stockman right away. Let's bring him in. And send units to—"

But her orders were cut off by a loud rumbling. Everyone froze, listening, wondering where the ominous sound was coming from. . . .

CHAPTER 21

Even in the Turtles' lair, deep below the streets, the rumbling could be heard and *felt*—vibrations shook dust and dirt from the ceiling onto the Turtles. The four brothers slowly moved from their separate spots, coming back together, gathering with Master Splinter around Donnie's workstation.

"What's happening up there, Donnie?" Leo asked.

On his monitors, Donnie brought up images from cameras all over the city. A swirling storm of energy was forming in the sky. The wind blew signs and lampposts, bending them. Lightning crackled out of the rotating storm.

"Not cool," Mikey said, staring at the eerie images.

In the sky above New York City, multiplying storm clouds formed a whirlpool, spinning around a growing rift in the fabric of space and time. The portal was opening . . .

. . . and the Technodrome came streaming through the dimensional passageway in thousands of chunks, like puzzle pieces, which came together, assembling themselves into a massive structure in the twisting sky.

A little girl pointed up at the Technodrome. "What is that, Mommy?"

"I don't know, baby," the mother said, scooping up her daughter and running away. All over the city, citizens panicked at the sight of the huge alien craft, letting out terrified cries and running for shelter.

Except for one construction worker, who glanced up and then went back to work. "Eh," he grunted. "Seen worse."

In the lair, Donnie said, "These images suggest some sort of alien craft. Its commanding officer goes by the name of Kraang."

Splinter and the others stared at the monitors, horrified by the scenes of chaos in the city they loved.

"I don't know that guy," Mikey said, "but I hate that guy."

Donnie checked a reading. "The atmosphere surrounding the portal would be toxic to anyone with a standard cardiovascular system."

"What are you saying?" Leo asked.

"That we may be the only ones who can survive around that portal. The only ones who can get close enough to the alien craft to shut it down."

The four Turtles considered the weight of what Donnie was saying: they might be the only ones who could save the world.

"But we're being hunted," Mikey pointed out. "They think we're monsters."

Raphael agreed. "We need the cops at our back, not trying to lock us up. Which isn't going to happen."

Donnie had an idea. "Unless . . . ," he said, pulling out the canister of purple ooze. It was now glowing.

He handed the canister to Leo. "One sip and each of us will . . . become human."

Leo and the others instinctively turned to their sensei for guidance. But Master Splinter said, "Your boyhood is drawing to an end. You're becoming young men. The choice is yours."

Leo looked at his three brothers. "I'll do whatever you guys say. It's your call."

He held the canister out to Raph. Without saying it, Leo was admitting he'd been wrong when he'd said only his vote counted. And Raph knew it.

After a moment, Raph took the canister from Leo. He considered it, weighing it in his hand. Then he turned and hurled it at the rock wall, smashing the canister into a thousand pieces.

They were Turtles. And Turtles they would remain.

CHAPTER
22

Over the city, another large section of the Technodrome slammed into place. It looked as though the alien craft would be shaped like a crescent moon when it was finished.

In a high-rise office building, employees gasped as gigantic pieces of the Technodrome zoomed by their windows. In one of those pieces, had it been slower, they could have caught a glimpse of Kraang relishing his arrival in their dimension.

At police headquarters, there was frenzied activity as police officers took calls from terrified citizens and organized their forces to respond to the growing threat.

"I want operational scenarios on how to get

that thing out of the sky!" Chief Vincent told Jade.

"On it!" Jade replied.

April, Casey, and Vern stood nearby. April's phone rang. She checked the caller ID and saw that it was Donnie. She turned to Vincent and said, "Just a guess, but this call is going to be about exactly that."

A few minutes later, April, Casey, Vern, Chief Vincent, Jade, and several police officers stood in an alley, waiting. The cops looked tense, with their guns drawn. Overhead, the Technodrome loomed in the darkened sky.

"You're sure they're coming?" Vincent asked.

"They're coming," April assured her.

A manhole cover rose. One by one, the Turtles emerged, looking strong, confident, and proud of who they were.

The cops aimed their guns, but Vincent raised her hand. "Hold your fire!" They all stared, amazed at what they were seeing.

"What . . . are you?" Vincent asked.

"They're mutant teenage turtle ninjas," Vern explained. "No, wait—that doesn't sound right. . . ."

Mikey stepped forward. "We're not really into labels."

"Some call us freaks or monsters," Leo said, stepping forward.

"But just consider us four brothers from New York who hate bullies and love our city," Raph said, joining his brothers.

"And right now," Donnie finished, stepping up, "we're the city's best hope."

Vincent looked skeptical. "And why should I believe you?"

"You don't have to take it from us," Leo said. "Take it from him." He nodded toward Vern.

All eyes turned to Vern. He didn't know what to say. He knew the Turtles deserved the whole city's gratitude and respect. But on the other hand, he *loved* being the Falcon.

"Tell her, Vern," April said. "Tell the chief the truth about the arrangement."

"Arrangement?" Vern asked, playing dumb.

Raph scowled at Vern, making a low growl in his throat.

"Oh, *that* arrangement!" Vern said. "Well, you see, the Falcon is still the Falcon, but I get by with a little help from my friends." He sighed. Time to spill the beans. "These four are really the ones who took down Shredder the first time. I was more of the . . . wingman. They've always had the city's best interests at heart."

April took a step toward Vincent. "So if you're looking for heroes"—she gestured toward the Turtles—"you don't need to look any further than these four."

Leo addressed the chief. "We're not heroes. We *have* been doing our part to protect the city from the shadows. And we think we have something to offer."

Raph clapped a hand on Leo's shoulder. "Strategy."

Leo looked at Raph. "Instinct."

Mikey nodded toward Donnie. "Logic."

Donnie put his hand on Mikey's shoulder. "And boatloads of heart."

The four brothers stood together, united as an unbreakable team, accepting each member's unique strengths. They were ready to take on any challenge.

Including Kraang and his Technodrome.

Vincent nodded. "Okay. Let's see what you can do."

Mikey grinned. "I'm just gonna go ahead and say it—*COWABUNGA!*"